Kaya's

Short Story
Collection

BELONGS TO

DATE

Read all of the novels about Kaya:

The adventures of *Kaya* continue in this keepsake collection of short stories. Kaya's a Nez Perce girl growing up before America became a country. She dreams of becoming a leader for her people, and she works hard to learn the lessons of her elders and to bravely meet the changes facing her people. Kaya's strong spirit, and her resolve to do her best, guide her.

Discover more about Kaya's world in these heartwarming stories of daring adventure and deeply held traditions.

Kaya's
SHORT STORY
COLLECTION

By JANET SHAW

ILLUSTRATIONS BY BILL FARNSWORTH

VIGNETTES BY SUSAN McALILEY

Published by Pleasant Company Publications
Copyright © 2006 by American Girl, LLC

Questions or comments? Call 1-800-845-0005,
visit our Web site at **americangirl.com**, or write to Customer Service,
American Girl, 8400 Fairway Place, Middleton, WI 53562-0497.

Printed in China
06 07 08 09 10 11 LEO 12 11 10 9 8 7 6 5 4 3 2 1

Cataloging-in-Publication Data
available from the Library of Congress.

TABLE OF CONTENTS

KAYA'S FAMILY
AND FRIENDS

TOE-TA
*Kaya's father, an
expert horseman and
wise village leader*

EETSA
*Kaya's mother, who is a
good provider for her
family and her village*

KAYA
*An adventurous girl
with a generous spirit*

KAUTSA
*Eetsa's mother, who
guides and comforts Kaya*

SPEAKING RAIN
*A blind girl who lives
with Kaya's family and
is a sister to Kaya*

BROWN DEER
*Kaya's sister, who is
old enough to court*

**WING FEATHER
AND SPARROW**
*Kaya's mischievous
twin brothers*

STEPS HIGH
Kaya's beloved horse

SPOTTED OWL
*A river girl who befriends
Speaking Rain*

BENT BOW
*A troubled boy who
Kaya tries to help*

WHITE BRAIDS
*A kind Salish
woman who saves
Speaking Rain's life*

TAAMAMNO
*An old grandmother
who teaches Kaya
an important lesson*

Kaya and her family are *Nimíipuu*,
known today as Nez Perce Indians.
They speak the Nez Perce
language, so you'll see some
Nez Perce words in this book.
"Kaya" is short for the Nez Perce
name *Kaya'aton'my'*, which means
"she who arranges rocks." You'll
find the meanings of these and
other Nez Perce words in the
glossary on pages 236–237.

KAYA AND THE RIVER GIRL

KAYA AND
THE RIVER GIRL

Kaya sat with her sister Speaking Rain on a plateau above the Big River. Tatlo lay beside Kaya, his pink tongue lolling. Speaking Rain was blind and couldn't play running games, but Kaya and the other girls had just finished a game of Shinny. Even though a strong wind blew up the river gorge, the summer evening was warm, and Kaya was hot and tired. As she rested, she worked on her toy horse. The little horse had legs of willow

1

sticks, a body of deerskin
stuffed with buffalo hair, and
a twist of buffalo hair for a tail.
Speaking Rain had twined hemp
cord to tie on the small saddle that Kaya
had fashioned from bent willow twigs.
The sisters loved working together.

"I'm coming to talk to you, *Nimíipuu*
girl!" a girl shouted to Kaya across the
playing field. "I want to ask you something!"

"Who's calling to you?" Speaking
Rain asked. "I don't recognize her voice."

Kaya looked up curiously at the girl
running toward her. "She's one of the
River People who live on the north shore,"
Kaya said. "We beat her and her friends

2

at Shinny. I don't know her name."

The girl halted beside Kaya and dropped to her knees. She had a pretty, round face with full lips and flashing eyes. A glowing copper bead was strung on the hemp cord she wore around her neck. "I'm Spotted Owl," she said, reaching out to stroke Kaya's toy horse. "I don't know your name, but I know you're a fast runner."

"Katsee-yow-yow," Kaya said. She felt her warm face grow warmer at the compliment. "I'm Kaya. My sister is Speaking Rain. How did you learn to speak our language so well?"

"My mother's a trading partner with a Nimíipuu woman. I've often traveled upstream with my mother to trade with

3

*"I'm Spotted Owl," she said, reaching out
to stroke Kaya's toy horse.*

her partner, or she's come downstream to us, especially now during salmon fishing season." Spotted Owl jumped to her feet again. "I came to find you because I want us to race! Will you run against me?"

Speaking Rain clasped Kaya's arm. "Go on, race her, Kaya!"

Tatlo's tail thumped against Kaya's leg as if he were urging her to race, too.

Kaya loved to run races, and she often won, even against the boys. She'd seen that Spotted Owl was a fast runner in Shinny—it would be a good test to run against her. *Aa-heh,* let's race," Kaya said. "Our friends can set out the markers."

Quickly the girls gathered again on the playing field. They laid several white

stones across the center of the field.
From that centerline they walked
a hundred paces toward each
end of the field, where they
placed other stones to mark
starting points. "I'll be the starter,"
Little Fawn cried. "Take your places!"

Spotted Owl took her place at one
end of the field. Kaya gave her pup to
Speaking Rain, then stood at the opposite
end of the field, facing her opponent.
Little Fawn raised her hand. When she
brought it down, both girls took off to
see who could cross the centerline first.

Kaya's heart was beating hard and
fast as she raced down the field.
Spotted Owl was coming swiftly, her

arms pumping, but Kaya felt so much strength in her legs that she knew she'd cross the finish line first. She was shocked to see Spotted Owl plunge across the line before she could reach it.

Kaya halted herself in a few steps and bent over, dragging in gasps of air. She heard the girls congratulating Spotted Owl. Just then, Tatlo bounded up and began licking Kaya's flaming face with his rough tongue. He seemed to be telling her that it didn't matter that she'd lost the race. But losing hurt her pride.

"Good race!" Spotted Owl called to her. "Let's have another one soon!"

Kaya knew she should praise Spotted Owl, but all Kaya could murmur

was "Aa-heh." She stayed bent over,
gazing at the ground, until the others had
left. Then she went dejectedly to sit with
Speaking Rain.

"I wish you'd won, but I like that
girl," Speaking Rain said. "She has a
strong spirit, don't you think?"

Kaya didn't answer. Her sister's

words only added to her injured pride. She vowed to become stronger, to practice racing every time she went for water or wood or to help with the horses. She vowed that the next time she and Spotted Owl raced, she would win.

When Speaking Rain went across the river to stay with White Braids, her Salish mother, for a little while, Kaya missed her sister badly. After a few sleeps, Kaya crossed the river to meet Speaking Rain. Working to get stronger, Kaya ran all the way upstream to where the Salish camped. She found Speaking Rain sitting in the shade of a tepee. At her side sat Spotted Owl. They were playing with their dolls.

"Tawts may-we!" Spotted Owl greeted

Kaya as she came close.

Kaya was taken aback to find the girl she thought of as her rival playing with her sister, but she didn't want to let her bruised feelings show. "Tawts may-we," she said politely to Spotted Owl. "Tawts may-we, Sister!" she said much more warmly to Speaking Rain.

"Spotted Owl comes to see me every day!" Speaking Rain said. "She just asked if I'd like to go with her to her village to visit She Who Watches, the old chief who looks after her people. I'd like to go, wouldn't you?"

Kaya saw that Speaking Rain wore Spotted Owl's necklace with the copper bead. "That's a pretty necklace,"

Kaya said quietly.

"Aa-heh, Spotted Owl gave it to me," Speaking Rain said.

Spotted Owl smiled up at Kaya in her easy, open way. "Kaya, won't you come with us? It's very good to visit She Who Watches. The spirits are very strong at the place where she guards over my people."

"Come with us," Speaking Rain urged.

Kaya wouldn't refuse her sister's request, but she wished she could just grasp Speaking Rain's hand and lead her away from Spotted Owl. Kaya had only just been reunited with her sister, and Speaking Rain spent part of her time with White Braids, who had saved her life. Kaya knew it was selfish, but she didn't

want to share what little time she and
Speaking Rain had with this river girl.

Spotted Owl didn't seem to notice
Kaya's chilly silence as they walked
downstream. She was busy telling
the story of She Who Watches.

"A long time ago, in the time
before memories, my people had
a woman chief," Spotted Owl began.

"A woman?" Speaking Rain asked.
"Nimíipuu have many women leaders,
but our chiefs are always men."

"Our chiefs are men, too, now. But
this was long ago," Spotted Owl continued.
"Our chief was wise and kind and firm,
and my people revered her. Then
one day Coyote disguised himself in a

12

bearskin and came up the river to our village. He wanted to find out if my people were grateful for all he'd taught them and the gifts he'd given them.

"Coyote walked through the village beside our chief. He saw that the people had built warm lodges and had plenty to eat. They were rich with goods that others had traded to them for the salmon they'd caught. All seemed well, but our chief felt a shiver of fear. She guessed that the creature in the bearskin was Coyote and that he might try to trick her.

"When Coyote asked if she treated her people well, she kept her voice steady to show her courage. 'You've seen all that my people and I have accomplished together,' she said. 'You've seen that my people respect me. Most important of all, I teach my people to do good.'

"Coyote leaned forward, and the bearskin slipped off his head. 'Listen to me!' he growled. 'You've done well for your people, but the world on the river is going to change. New people will come, bringing great sickness and death. You will no longer be chief. Indeed, there will be no more women chiefs for your people.'

"'I will stay here as long as my people want me to lead them!' our chief said firmly.

"'Then it will be as you wish,' Coyote growled. 'Your time has come to an end, but nothing will separate you from your people. Your name shall be She Who Watches, and you'll guard your people for all the years to come. This will be so!' Then Coyote slipped away, and no one has seen him since.

"When people went looking for our chief, she had vanished. They found instead a strange new face chipped into a pillar of rock—it was She Who Watches. And she's still guarding us after all these years," Spotted Owl said, finishing her story.

After a time the girls reached the place where She Who Watches looked out over the River People's village and across the wide river beyond. Kaya drew in a sharp breath when she looked up into the face of the old chief, still reminding her

15

people to do good and live well.

"What do you see, Kaya?" Speaking Rain asked. "Tell me."

Kaya led her sister forward until they stood beneath the face etched into the reddish-gray basalt. "She's up there, higher than the tallest tepee pole," Kaya said. Then she stretched Speaking Rain's arms wide. "Her face is broader than your outstretched arms. Her eyes are huge and wide. She sees everything."

Speaking Rain raised her face toward the painted image above them. "Her eyes are made of stone, but she's not blind like me," she said softly.

"She sees with her heart, just as you do," Spotted Owl said kindly to Speaking Rain.

*Kaya drew in a sharp breath when she looked up into the face
of the old chief.*

17

"My sister is the kindest person that I know!" Kaya exclaimed. She wanted to be the one to praise her sister, not this river girl. After all, Kaya knew Speaking Rain better than anyone else did.

Spotted Owl didn't seem to notice Kaya's cold tone of voice. "Come have a meal with us," she said. "My mother's going to cook a big salmon that my father caught this morning. It will be delicious!"

"Katsee-yow-yow!" Speaking Rain said with pleasure.

"Katsee-yow-yow," Kaya echoed in a grim voice that hardly seemed her own. *Why can't I feel the way my sister does about this good-natured girl?* she asked herself.

18

Kaya looked up again at the wide, wise eyes of She Who Watches. Could the old chief show her some way to get rid of these painful feelings that she knew were wrong?

But Kaya's bad feelings about Spotted Owl didn't disappear. When Speaking Rain praised her new friend, Kaya kept quiet. When her sister said she hoped Spotted Owl would come back and race again, Kaya bit her lip. She hoped she wouldn't have to think about Spotted Owl once the salmon runs were over and Kaya's band left the Big River.

One evening several canoes of River People crossed to the south side of the river for trading and games. A group of girls gathered at the playing field for a game of Shinny. Before the game began, Spotted Owl ran to greet Speaking Rain. But when Spotted Owl called a greeting to Kaya, Kaya pretended not to hear.

The river girls played hard and well, scoring two goals right away. Kaya tried even harder to help her team get ahead. The running she'd done had made her legs stronger, and she took the ball as often as she could, hoping to score a goal.

Kaya was racing with the ball out ahead of the others when Spotted Owl caught up with her. With a swift jab of her stick, Spotted Owl scooped the ball away from Kaya. "No you don't!" Kaya cried.

As she hurled herself after her opponent, Kaya shoved her stick between Spotted Owl's feet to try to get the ball back. Spotted Owl tripped on the stick, and Kaya bumped into her, pushing her to the ground and knocking the air out of her. Spotted Owl's teammates helped her off the field so she could catch her breath.

Alarmed that she'd hurt Spotted Owl in anger, Kaya went miserably to sit with Speaking Rain. For a time the girls sat in silence as Kaya struggled with her shame. "It's my fault Spotted Owl got hurt," Kaya finally admitted. "I've had bad feelings about her. Everything she does and says is good, yet I feel as if she's my enemy!"

Speaking Rain put her hand on Kaya's

shoulder. "Listen to me," she said gently.
"It's true that Spotted Owl's a good person.
In what she says and does, she's so much
like you, Sister! You're both leaders.
You're both strong. But we mustn't be
like coyotes, who hunt alone. Our grandmother always tells us that we must be like
wolves—strong individually, but always
working together. She Who Watches must
have taught that to her people, too."

Kaya rested her chin on her knees as
she considered her sister's wise words.
Slowly her churning feelings smoothed
and she knew what she had to do. "I have
to go after Spotted Owl," she murmured
as she got to her feet.

Kaya put a horsehair rope on the chestnut mare that was staked near the tepees. Then she rode upstream to where the River People had beached their canoes. Some traders were already loading their canoes for the return crossing. Kaya scanned the crowd for Spotted Owl, but she wasn't there. Kaya rode farther upstream.

Around the bend, Kaya saw a strong-looking elder woman seated in the stern of her heavily loaded canoe. Spotted Owl was pushing out Elder Woman's canoe so that she could cross back to the other side.

Kaya dismounted and walked up the

shore toward Spotted Owl. As Kaya wondered what she could say to make things right, she watched Elder Woman's progress.

Elder Woman expertly guided the big canoe into the swift current. She pointed its bow upstream into the current so that she could ferry the canoe sideways to the opposite shore. But when the canoe was gliding by a rocky outcropping, her paddle struck underwater rocks. In an instant the paddle was snapped from her grip. Elder Woman leaned out, trying to grab her paddle. Kaya gasped when the force of the current tilted the canoe, tossing Elder Woman into the water.

Elder Woman was washed against the

outcropping. She tried to scramble up and away from the heavy canoe bearing down on her, pushed by the mighty river. Kaya watched in horror as the canoe plowed against Elder Woman's leg, smashing her against the rocks. Elder Woman cried out.

The powerful current dragged the canoe around the end of the outcropping and swept it downstream. Elder Woman clung to the outcropping, but she seemed to be in so much pain that Kaya worried she might pass out and be carried away by the rushing river.

Both Kaya and Spotted Owl knew that they had to work fast to rescue Elder Woman. The girls ran to another, smaller canoe nearby. They shoved the canoe into

25

the water, climbing in as it moved away from shore. In the stern, Spotted Owl angled the bow slightly upstream, and they swept sideways out to where Elder Woman was stranded. Kaya could see Elder Woman's arms trembling as she struggled to hold on to the rocks.

Spotted Owl guided the canoe into the calm water on the downstream side of the outcropping, where she held the canoe still. *I must be strong!* Kaya thought as she climbed swiftly from the prow onto the rocks toward Elder Woman. Just before Kaya could reach her, Elder Woman lost her grip on the slippery rocks and began to go under. Kaya lunged, seized the woman under her arms, and pulled with

all her might, tearing Elder Woman from
the churning waters. Kaya half-dragged
and half-carried her across the rocks to the
canoe. Elder Woman cried out again as
Kaya eased her over the side and jumped
in after her. Spotted Owl ferried them back
to shore, where other women had gathered.

"Take my horse!" Kaya cried as the

women lifted Elder Woman from the canoe. Quickly, they lashed a travois to the horse and helped Elder Woman onto it. They led the horse downstream to get aid for Elder Woman's injured leg.

Kaya's heart was thudding and her arms aching from the effort of the rescue. Spotted Owl's face was red and sweat ran into her eyes. But when their gazes met, they both smiled. "We worked well together," Spotted Owl said.

"Aa-heh, we did," Kaya agreed.

The girls splashed cold river water onto their faces. As Kaya wiped her eyes, a good thought came to her. "I want you to have my toy horse."

"I like that horse!" Spotted Owl said. "I'll trade you my doll for it."

"That's a fine trade," Kaya agreed. "Listen to me. You and I could be trading partners. Would you like that?"

When Spotted Owl nodded happily, Kaya took a deep breath. She felt as if she'd been underwater for a long, long time and now, at last, she could lift her head into the air again. She couldn't wait to tell Speaking Rain all that had happened and how she and Spotted Owl had worked together and become friends—for Kaya was certain that this was what She Who Watches must have wanted.

LOOKING BACK

TRADING IN 1764

This late-nineteenth-century photo shows the massive falls at Celilo.

In Kaya's time, tens of thousands of people from all over the Northwest gathered each summer to trade, fish, and socialize along the Columbia River at Celilo Falls. Some came from as far away as modern-day Montana, while others traveled east from the Pacific Ocean.

Spotted Owl's people, the Wishram, did not have to travel far at all. They were one of several tribes who set up permanent villages along the river.

Each tribe brought a different item to trade. Kaya's people traveled throughout the year, and they brought roasted camas roots from the high meadows. Spotted Owl's people lived along the river year round and offered dried salmon and salmon eggs to tribes who lived too far away from the river to fish.

Fresh salmon was smoked over a low fire.

Nez Perce baskets (left) were decorated with triangles, diamonds, and other geometric shapes to represent trees, mountains, and other landmarks in nature. Wishram baskets (right) also featured human and animal figures.

Baskets were common trade items for all tribes from the plateau region, including the Nez Perce and the Wishram. Baskets were used for gathering, storing, and preparing food. Tightly woven baskets could even be used to carry water.

Girls like Kaya and Spotted Owl began to learn how to weave when they were only about six years old. A girl's first basket, whether it was good or bad, was always given to an older, accomplished basket maker in her village or tribe. This was done out of respect and to help bring the girl luck in her future as a basket maker.

The Wishram were widely known for their unique round or flat twined bags made from dried beargrass and hemp. Women and girls used dried berries and plants to make dyes to color the materials they used to make their baskets.

Women also dried berries for food and for trade.

Many of the designs that were woven into baskets were also seen in ancient rock art on the bluffs above the Columbia River. No one knows for sure who made these early artworks, but the artists used their art to record what happened in their world, their beliefs, and their legends.

Rock art is commonly found in places, like Celilo Falls, where people gathered to trade and fish. These designs may have been created to mark a specific location

or as a special symbol, such as to show appreciation for the many fish that gave themselves for food.

Besides trading and fishing, the summer gathering at the Falls gave Kaya's and Spotted Owl's families a chance to see old friends and make new ones. Since every tribe spoke a different language, communicating was sometimes a challenge. Many people used sign language— a language

Rock art designs ranged from simple wavy lines to detailed images, including animals, hunters, and mythical beings like She Who Watches.

of hand symbols that people from most tribes could understand.

Those who had a trading partner in another tribe often learned the language of their trading partner. Spotted Owl spoke Kaya's language because her mother had a Nez Perce trading partner and had learned to talk with her.

Trading partners exchanged gifts every time they saw each other. Each summer at Celilo Falls, and at other times throughout the

Young girls traded with girls their age from other tribes.

year, the partners traded woven bags or baskets, food, or maybe toys or clothing. Trading partners always knew they were welcome in the other's tribe. They often hunted or fished in each other's areas, and sometimes they even arranged marriages between their children!

Trading partners were truly friends for life. Kaya and Spotted Owl's trade of the toy horse and doll might have been the first of many exchanges between the two friends.

Nez Perce girls today still learn traditional basket making.

KAYA AND
THE BEAVERS

KAYA AND
THE BEAVERS

Kaya ran silently over grassy sedge iced white with frost, her fur-lined moccasins leaving faint tracks on it. Dressed warmly in deerskin shirts, Sparrow and Wing Feather ran right behind her. Though the twins were in only their fifth winter, they were strong and good runners. They stayed close to Kaya as they climbed into the foothills above their winter village.

In this cold season *Eetsa* often asked

43

Kaya to take the boys out of the smoky, crowded longhouse so they could get fresh air and burn off energy. Today the sky was clear and blue and there was no wind, so Kaya had decided to take the twins to a place she'd discovered farther up the valley. She'd told them a surprise waited for them there.

"Are we almost to the surprise you promised?" Sparrow called to her.

"She said we should whisper!" Wing Feather chided his twin.

Kaya glanced back at the boys, their breath white puffs at their lips. "Aa-heh," she whispered. "We don't want to scare away the surprise!" She let the boys catch

44

up to her, and slowed them to a walk as they came nearer to the top of the hill.

"If we could scare it, the surprise must be an animal," Sparrow guessed.

"Or birds?" Wing Feather asked.

"Remember, whisper!" Sparrow bumped his brother with his shoulder.

With both hands spread, palms down, Kaya threw them the words *Quiet down!* She led them over the rise and along the steep slope to a thicket of shrub willows. The boys crept into the thicket at her heels, their lips pressed tightly together. Kaya slowly pushed back branches to create an opening, and they peered through.

A clear stream ran from the upland end of the valley, widening into a large

pond below where they hid. On the far
shore of the pond sat a beaver lodge,
shaped like a squat tepee. It
jutted out into the water, a
dense thicket protecting it
from behind. Sitting at
some distance from the
lodge, the beaver dam
was constructed of sticks
and mud, like the lodge.

The blue surface of the pond was
marked by ripples made by a large beaver
as it swam back and forth alongside the
dam. Kaya and her brothers could clearly
see the beaver's furry face, his small dark
eyes, and the top of his long, dark brown
body as he swam.

"Tawts!" Sparrow said in a hushed voice. "The surprise is a beaver!"

"A family of beavers!" Kaya whispered. "That's the one I call Old Scout. He's inspecting the dam, looking for places where it needs to be repaired."

Another large beaver surfaced outside of the lodge and swam about in front of it. "That's Old Scout's mate," Kaya said quietly. "I call her Brings a Branch because she's so good at felling trees."

Right behind Brings a Branch, two other beavers swam out of the underwater entranceway to the lodge. They were lighter in color and smaller than the two adults. "Those are their kits," Kaya whispered. "I call them Dip and Dive.

They want to play all the time, like you two bothersome boys!"

"How did you find them, Kaya?" Sparrow asked.

"They helped me gather firewood," she said with a smile.

"Don't tease," Wing Feather said.

"But it's true," Kaya insisted. "I found twigs the beavers had clipped from the trees they'd felled. The twigs are good fire starters, so I started collecting them. Soon I found this pond." She pointed. "The beavers remind me of Nimíipuu. They make lodges like we do, and Old Scout's like our leader. He always looks after his people with strength and wisdom."

The boys were watching the kits

"We're like Dip and Dive!" Wing Feather said with a grin.

play in the water in front of the lodge. "We're like Dip and Dive!" Wing Feather said with a grin. "Look, they swim right toward each other and dive just before they crash." He shoved Sparrow with his shoulder, and his twin shoved back.

But again Kaya made the sign *Quiet down!*, for suddenly Old Scout stopped his patrol. He poised in the water with his head lifted and his nostrils working as he picked up a scent that troubled him. He studied the dam and the shoreline. Then, after a moment, he began swimming at top speed toward the far shore.

As Old Scout approached the end of the dam, he hissed a warning. Then he curled his broad, flat tail up over his back

and brought it down on the water with
a slap that sent up a geyser of spray and
made a sharp crack that echoed off the
hillsides.

The boys startled at the loud slap.
Though Kaya had heard
a beaver tail slap many
times, she startled, too. The
loud warning immediately
sent the other beavers diving out
of sight.

Kaya saw movement in the under-
brush. Was it a wolf? A bear? In another
moment a boy stepped out onto the shore.
It was Bent Bow, a scrawny boy of about
eight winters. His hair was tangled and
his thin arms were bare. He carried his

51

bow, and his quiver of arrows hung over his shoulder. Though he was young, he was known to be a good shot.

Bent Bow made his way a little distance down the shore toward the beaver lodge, but Old Scout hissed and slapped his tail again, sending the warning *Stay away!*

Bent Bow scowled at the old beaver. Then he picked up a stone, drew back his arm, and hurled the stone at Old Scout. Even before the stone hit the water, Old Scout dove under the surface and disappeared.

"He's a mean boy," Sparrow said, his arms folded across his chest. "He spooks the horses and kicks the dogs if they come close to him."

"He shot a fat grouse but just left it on the ground for crows to eat," Wing Feather said with disgust. "*Kautsa* told him he'd done wrong. She said a hunter must respect the birds and animals that give themselves to us for food."

"Bent Bow tried to blame us, but she knew he was lying," Sparrow added. "She called Whipman."

"Aa-heh," Wing Feather agreed. "We all got switched for his bad deed, but he wasn't sorry."

"He used to be a kind boy," Kaya said thoughtfully. "When he caught a salmon, he took it right away to his grandmother to cook. But that was before enemies from the south attacked his family when they were hunting. Bent Bow saw arrows strike his mother and father. Maybe those arrows injured Bent Bow's spirit."

"We don't trust him," Sparrow said. "We stay out of his way!"

"He's got his bow and arrows. He might shoot Old Scout just for target practice," Wing Feather warned.

"I don't think he would hunt the beavers—" Kaya began, but she pressed her fist to her lips and didn't go on. Old Scout sensed that the boy was a threat to him and his family. No Nimíipuu hunter would kill any creature needlessly. But maybe Bent Bow, in his dark and angry mood, might try to shoot the old beaver or his mate and kits. Her face grew hot as she imagined the beaver family in danger from this troubled boy. "I don't know what Bent Bow might do," Kaya admitted at last, "but the beavers are safe as long as they're in their lodge."

As she spoke, the boy picked up another stone and hurled it at the beaver lodge. The stone struck near the airhole in the top, then bounced off into the water. He shook his fist, then stepped back into the thicket and disappeared. "He's gone now," Kaya said softly. "Let's hope he stays far, far away from the beaver pond."

A few sleeps later, when Kaya looked

after Wing Feather and Sparrow again, they begged to go back to the beaver pond with her. They wanted to watch the beavers at their work and play. But Kaya wanted to see if Bent Bow had returned.

All looked well when she settled the boys into her viewing place with her. She saw the tracks of the beavers' paws in the mud along the shore. The drag marks of their heavy tails crisscrossed the beach. There were deer and raccoon tracks, too, but she didn't see any human footprints. *Tawts!* she thought. She hoped Bent Bow had lost interest in the beaver family.

Kaya and the twins pulled their deer-skins closely around their shoulders and settled down to watch for the beavers.

56

They didn't have long to wait. Soon Old Scout and then Brings a Branch emerged from their lodge through the underwater entrance and swam to the surface. A moment later the kits followed.

The boys held back giggles as they watched Dip and Dive play in front of the lodge. The young beavers dove and surfaced in unison and slid over each other with soft splashes like river otters. Their dives sounded like canoe paddles entering the water. But Old Scout and Brings a Branch didn't cavort with their children— they set right to work.

Brings a Branch climbed ashore and sniffed a small birch tree. Then she seized the trunk in her shiny black paws and began tugging off strips of wood with her sharp teeth. In only a short time the tree began to tremble and creak. Brings a Branch hopped sideways to get out of the way as the birch fell to the ground with a hollow thump.

The kits heard the tree fall and swam to join their mother. They greeted her with chirps as they crept up the bank and rubbed noses with her. Then they settled down beside her to eat the delicate bark of the birch twigs.

"They share their food, just like we do," Kaya whispered to the boys.

Old Scout was on the far shore, dragging a small

aspen he'd felled toward the pond. When he had the tree in the water, he gripped it with his teeth at the chewed-off end so that it drifted alongside him as he swam to the food storage place near the lodge. Once there, he dove down with the little tree to anchor the trunk in the mud at the bottom of the pond.

The kits finished their meal and began clipping branches from the birch. Then they swam with the branches to the dam, where they shoved them over the top of the structure to make it stronger.

Kaya was admiring how well the kits worked when Sparrow grabbed her arm. He pointed toward the far shore. Wing Feather pointed, too. At first Kaya saw only Old Scout at work felling another aspen. Then she saw what the boys did. A large grizzly bear lurked in the shadows on the hillside!

"Don't move!" Kaya whispered to the boys. "We're downwind of the bear. He can't smell us, and he can't see us over here!"

The boys pressed against her as the bear repeatedly sniffed the air. In this season the bears were eating the last of the fish and berries before they entered their dens to sleep until spring. But the bear must have caught Old Scout's scent and decided that a meal of meat would be better than berries, for suddenly it charged down the slope after the fat beaver.

"Run, Old Scout!" Kaya breathed.
Old Scout went scrambling at top speed
toward the pond and safety. The bear was
fast, but the beaver managed to plunge
into the water and slide beneath the surface just ahead of the grizzly's long claws
and sharp teeth.

When Kaya looked for the other
beavers, they had fled and were out of
sight. She guessed that they'd returned to
their lodge.

The bear swung its head from side
to side, gazing all around with
its black eyes. Then it started
through the thicket toward the
beaver lodge. The bushes of the
thicket were densely intertwined, but the

bear crashed through them until it reached the lodge. Then it clambered up onto it. Growling, it forced its nose into the opening.

"The bear's trying to break in!" Sparrow whispered.

"It'll kill the beavers!" Wing Feather cried.

"Listen to me," Kaya said firmly to the twins. "The bear might damage the lodge, but it can't catch the beavers. By now they've slipped out from one of the underwater entrances and are long gone. Look, the bear's leaving now. It realizes they've escaped!"

Kaya heard a twig snap behind her. She peeked out of the viewing place. The twins peered out, too, then shrank back down. For there, standing a little way up the slope, was Bent Bow. His face was contorted in an ugly scowl. He held his bow tightly, his knuckles white. He'd been watching the bear chase Old Scout, too.

"We think the beavers got away," Kaya said quietly, hoping to calm the boy.

"I'm not troubled about them!" Bent Bow said in a strangled voice. "Maybe the beavers can escape, but my parents were surrounded by our enemies. They didn't have a chance!"

Kaya saw that Bent Bow's face was dark with anger. Did it hurt to know that the beavers could save themselves when his parents hadn't been able to?

Kaya saw that Bent Bow's face was dark with anger.

Kaya reached toward Bent Bow. But he ran off into the trees and was out of sight.

Kaya got slowly to her feet, and the twins stood, too. The bear had gone back into the woods, and the surface of the pond was smooth. The beavers were probably hiding in the marshy waters where they couldn't be seen. All seemed quiet now, but Kaya's skin prickled with dread.

"I think Bent Bow was glad that the bear attacked the beaver lodge!" Wing Feather said with a frown.

Kaya had been thinking the same thing. Perhaps Bent Bow could be as much of a threat to the beavers as a hungry bear.

During the night the northeast wind came up and the cold deepened. When Kaya went to the stream to get water, she saw pieces of ice floating downstream on the current. In weather like this, the beaver pond would soon freeze over.

After Kaya took the water to the longhouse, she headed to the beaver pond to see how much ice had formed on it. She knew the beavers could break an opening through the ice by bumping it from beneath. But in a few sleeps, the ice would be too thick to break. Then the beavers would stay in their lodge, swimming out beneath the ice to get to their underwater food supply. It came to Kaya that perhaps the beavers would be safer then. Bent Bow, and other predators, wouldn't be able to reach them to do them harm.

As she climbed toward the rise that overlooked the pond, she heard something that made her catch her breath. She stopped to listen. What was that sound? With a shock she realized that she heard the frightening drone of fast-flowing water.

Kaya knew that the level of the pond must stay high as the cold season came on. If the pond became too shallow, it would freeze solid all the way to the bottom. The beavers wouldn't be able to swim to the food supply they'd stored there. Trapped in their lodge all winter without food, they'd starve. And now the pond was draining away!

In a panic Kaya raced down the slope toward the broken dam. In her haste she stumbled and went to her knees, but she got up and ran on. When she reached the dam, she stepped cautiously onto the wet mud and sticks. From here she saw that the water churned through the broken place with great force. It gushed out in a wild stream, pulling away sticks and logs and sending them cascading downhill in the current. Every moment the break in the dam was getting larger.

Had the grizzly returned and

damaged the beavers' dam? She looked
for bear tracks in the mud near the broken
place, but instead of claw marks she saw
human footprints.

She whirled around and caught sight
of Bent Bow crouching in the tall grass
beside the pond, his bow over his shoulder. When he realized that she'd seen him
there, he started running. *Bent Bow did
this!* Kaya thought, her chest hot.

Bent Bow was a fast runner, but
Kaya's anger gave her strength. She
chased the boy up the frosty hillside, and
just over the top she caught up to him.
Seizing his arm, she swung him around to
face her. "Why did you smash the dam?"
she cried.

The boy's dark eyes were only slits. "I didn't smash it!" he hissed.

"I saw your footprints on it!" Kaya cried, keeping a tight grip on his arm. "You ripped out some logs, didn't you?"

"*Wah-tu*, I did not!" Bent Bow shook his head fiercely in denial.

"There's mud on your moccasins, and on your hands, too!" Kaya insisted.

Bent Bow yanked his arm from Kaya's grip. His mouth turned down, and his face seemed to crumple.

"Admit it!" Kaya was shaking with anger at this act of destruction.

Bent Bow lowered his head. "Aa-heh, I broke it," he choked out. "But it was an accident!"

"How can you destroy a dam by accident?" Kaya asked bitterly.

"I didn't mean to," Bent Bow said, his words coming slowly. "I wanted to put another log on the dam—I wanted to help the beaver family."

"You didn't help the beavers by throwing rocks at them. I saw you!" Kaya cried.

Bent Bow dropped his chin to his chest. "I was mad that day because the old beaver wouldn't let me get close to him or the others. They reminded me of my family . . ." His voice trailed off.

Kaya was silent for a few moments before she spoke again. "What happened to the dam?"

"I tried to shove my log in with the other logs," Bent Bow went on. "I pushed hard! Then my log knocked some mud and sticks loose, and they fell down the back of the dam. When I tried to grab the sticks, I knocked off more. All of a sudden, water was rushing out, and I couldn't stop it! It tore loose more and more sticks! I didn't mean to smash the dam, but now it's too late!"

Kaya believed him when he said he was sorry for what he'd done. Poor, unhappy boy! She remembered Kautsa's wise words that she'd repeated many, many times—Nimíipuu must always help each other. But what could Kaya do to help the boy—and what could the two of them do to help the beavers?

"Come with me!" she said. She began to run back toward the dam, Bent Bow right at her heels.

The rapidly emptying beaver pond wrenched her heart. The water was running out so swiftly that now the underwater entryways to the beaver lodge were beginning to show above the waterline. Soon the exposed lodge would stand like a defenseless tepee on the mud. A wolf or bear could easily get at the beavers.

Old Scout was swimming at top speed back and forth in front of the broken dam, checking the damage. Then he sped off to the far shore and quickly felled a willow shrub, which he floated across the pond to the broken place. He tipped the shrub over the crest of the dam and anchored it firmly between some rocks. When this held, he went back for more.

Brings a Branch had felled a sapling, too. She swam with it to the dam and tipped it over the crest beside Old Scout's shrub. The kits sped the length of the pond with sticks in their teeth. Nothing distracted their attention. They all knew their lives depended on fast action.

Kaya and Bent Bow watched as Old Scout and Brings a Branch felled bushes as quickly as possible and brought them to the dam. But the stream of water slowed only a little. The beavers had to cut down new trees to repair the dam, and it was taking a very long time. "If only they could build with the wood they've already cut!" Kaya whispered to Bent Bow.

"But that wood washed downstream," he said in a hopeless voice. He pointed to the gully below the dam where the beaver sticks were lodged like driftwood in the rocks.

"Aa-heh," Kaya said softly. Then she had an idea. "Listen to me," she said. "We can't help the beavers repair the dam—only they know how to do that. But we can carry up some of the sticks that washed away. If we can get their wood to them, they'll know how to use it. Will you help?"

Bent Bow didn't hesitate. "It's my fault that the dam's broken," he said. "I want to help fix it!" He flung down his bow and arrows and ran ahead of Kaya down the rocky hillside behind the dam.

In the gully Kaya and Bent Bow collected as many beaver sticks as they could carry. Climbing on the slippery stones, they toted the load back up to the dam. There they dumped the sticks into the water, where they floated near the shore. Though Kaya wasn't sure that the beavers would accept their offering, she and Bent Bow hurried back down the slope to gather more—it was all that they could do.

On their next trip up to the pond, Kaya saw something that raised her spirits high. Old Scout was swimming toward shore to fell another shrub when he suddenly discovered the cache of floating wood. Immediately he plunged into the midst of the tangled sticks, sniffing one branch after another and making excited cries. Then he seized a large stick in his teeth and sped with it to the broken place. There he crawled across the dam, mounted the crest, and toppled the stick into the breach. As he worked, he chirped about his find to the other beavers.

"Look!" Kaya whispered to Bent Bow. Now Brings a Branch and the kits were swimming to the floating cache, too. They set to work untangling sticks and taking them to repair the dam. As soon as they completed one trip, they began another. Now the work went quickly, for the beavers didn't have to cut down each tree before they used it.

Kaya and Bent Bow continued to haul driftwood up from the gully all day, adding it to the cache of wood in the pond. Their hands and arms were covered with mud, their legs ached from climbing on the slippery stones, and, despite the cold, sweat ran into their eyes. But they kept at it.

As the beavers worked, the flow of water from the break diminished to a thin stream, and the level of the pond began to rise a little. Kaya saw that now the beavers were building steadily but without haste. With this unexpected supply of wood, there was no need for them to panic.

As darkness approached, Kaya signaled for Bent Bow to join her on the shore of the pond. They watched the dark shapes of the beavers moving through the water. "We have to go back to our village," she said.

"But we could light a torch and keep working," Bent Bow urged her.

"We've done what we can for now," Kaya said.

Bent Bow wiped his face on the sleeve of his deerskin shirt. "That big beaver you call Brings a Branch reminds me of my mother," he said after a moment.

"We've done what we can for now," Kaya said

"Remember what a hard worker she was? Her *wyakin* was a beaver. It gave her the power to build good tepees for us."

"I remember," Kaya said. In the last light she could just make out the boy's face, but she heard the quiet, thoughtful tone of his voice. He'd done his best to mend the break he'd made with the beavers when he knocked a hole in their dam. And she was sure now that she'd done right to help him make amends. "We'll come back at sunup. I'm certain the beavers will mend their dam," she reassured him. *And,* Kaya thought, *I'm certain that you will mend your troubled spirit.*

LOOKING BACK

WORKING TOGETHER

This peaceful pond was formed after beavers built their dam.

Native Americans called the beaver the "sacred center" of the land. Like the Nimíipuu, who treated the land with respect, Old Scout and his family took good care of their environment. The flooded area behind their dam formed a

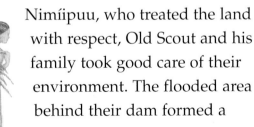

Kaya and other Nez Perce girls provided for their families by collecting firewood.

wetland habitat that was a perfect place for many other animals to live. Deer, fish, turtles, frogs, and ducks were able to thrive in and around the

Baby beavers help their parents build and repair dams and lodges.

pond. Kaya and her brothers were fond of watching Old Scout and his family because the beavers reminded them of their Nez Perce family.

The season of *Sek-le-wáal*, when trees dropped their leaves and cold came into the high country, was a time of preparation for winter. Kaya's people

A longhouse was home to several families—and sometimes the entire village!

constructed their longhouses in deep mountain valleys that sheltered them from the rough winds and heavy snows to come. At the same time, Old Scout and Brings a Branch added sticks to the roof of their lodge to strengthen it. They dove to the bottom of the pond and scooped up as much mud as they could carry beneath their chins. Back on the surface of the water, the busy beavers climbed the exterior of their lodge and coated it with the mud. As winter set in, the mud froze and became as hard as concrete. This repair work made their home safe from predators—

An adult beaver can cut down more than 200 trees in one year.

like hungry bears—that might try to claw through the top of the lodge.

Like the Nimíipuu, beavers gathered and stored food for the cold months. A beaver family—called a colony—would need 1,500 to 2,500 pounds of tree branches in their winter food pile to survive. Placing the pile as close to the lodge entrance as possible made it easier

Beavers keep warm in the winter by sleeping on top of one another.

for Dip and Dive to find the food in the almost-total darkness.

Beavers do not hibernate in the winter, but they are less active in their snow-covered lodges. The Nez Perce, on the other hand, were busy in their winter homes. Women made and mended clothes and wove baskets. Men crafted bows and arrows, nets for fishing, and horsehair ropes. Children helped with these chores, learning valuable skills and enjoying a quieter, closer time with family and friends. As they worked

around a crackling fire, they listened to
the elders tell stories and legends. Many
of the stories were about animals, which
were important teachers for children.
According to legend, long before there
were humans on the earth, animals could
talk, and they acted like people. Their
actions taught Kaya and her brothers
about the traditions and history of the

*Everything in the Nez Perce culture was passed on by example and
by stories and legends that the people learned by heart.*

Nez Perce people, about the behavior that was expected of them, and about the world around them.

Kaya and her brothers were able to enjoy the antics of Old Scout's family because, in their time, beavers were active during the day. That changed, however, when white men came to Nez Perce country and began hunting beavers in the early 1800s. Hats and coats made from beaver pelts were warm and held

up well under rugged conditions. Items made from beaver fur became so popular that by the late 1800s,

In the early 1800s, more than one hundred thousand beaver pelts were shipped to Europe each year to be made into hats.

beavers were almost extinct. To survive, beavers became *nocturnal*, or active only at night. Today they still sleep during the day. Trapping limits were set in the early 1900s, so beavers are no longer in danger of disappearing. If you discover a beaver pond at sunset, you just may see a furry family emerge from its lodge and begin a day of work and play.

When young beavers are a year old, they are called "yearlings." They stay with their parents until they are two years old so that they can help raise the next set of kits.

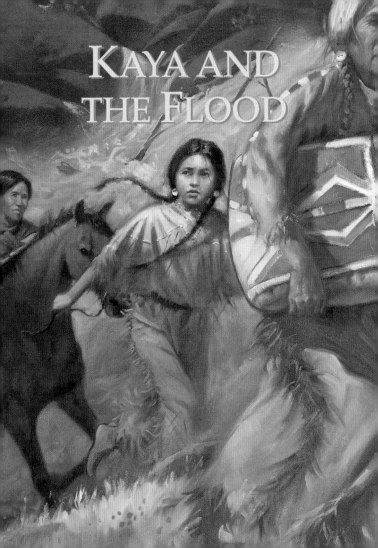

KAYA AND
THE FLOOD

KAYA AND
THE FLOOD

Kaya rode Steps High over a carpet of
flowers, the horse's colt, Sparks
Flying, trotting right behind. As Kaya
rode, she gazed happily at the yellow
bells, buttercups, and bluebells covering
the ground as far as the eye
could see. Spring had come
again, and once more Kaya's people were
on the move. She rode with many other
Nimíipuu, their belongings packed onto
horses, journeying away from their winter

village in Salmon River Country. Many
of the men and boys had gone northward
to fish and hunt. Most of the women and
girls were traveling to the Camas Prairie
to dig roots, for kouse plants grew thickly
there. The women had set up
camp with other bands, and for
many sleeps the diggers would fill
bag after bag with fresh roots to
nourish the people for the coming
year. Kaya was eager to be among the first
root diggers.

Last digging season, Kaya had kept
away from the roots so that her sad feelings about her mentor's death wouldn't
spoil the food. But now her time of
mourning was over. She reached into her

pack and touched the bone handle of her digging stick, made from a strong hawthorn limb. Kautsa had made this digging stick for her. As Kaya touched the fire-hardened tip, she felt filled with energy and purpose. Soon she'd be working with the others!

digging stick   As they rode into the canyon of Whitebird Creek, Kaya heard a sudden gasp from a woman riding behind her. Kaya turned in her saddle. Yellow Flower, a young mother with her little daughter seated behind her, was bent over in her saddle. She clutched the pommel with both hands, her lower lip caught in her teeth.

Kaya turned Steps

pommel of a saddle

High and rode back a few steps to the young mother's side. "Are you troubled about something?" she asked respectfully.

Yellow Flower took a deep breath and pressed both hands against her swollen belly. "I thought this baby would wait to be born until we were settled at the Camas Prairie," she said in a low voice. "But it seems this baby doesn't want to wait." Again, Yellow Flower bit her lip and bent forward. After a moment, she murmured, "I don't think I can ride much farther."

"I'll get Kautsa," Kaya said. Her grandmother was an experienced midwife and medicine woman who had helped many women give birth to their babies. Kaya cantered up the trail to catch up with her grandmother, who rode near the head of the line of other riders and pack horses.

When she saw Kaya, Kautsa reined in her chestnut mare and motioned for the other women to come to a halt, too. "This is no time for a horse race, so you must have something to tell me, Granddaughter," Kautsa said.

"Ah-heh, Kautsa," Kaya said. "Yellow Flower says her baby is ready to be born, and she isn't able to ride any farther."

Kautsa frowned. She signaled Kaya's mother to accompany them, and the three rode back to talk with Yellow Flower, who sat slumped on her horse on the sandbar.

Kaya watched her grandmother lean close to Yellow Flower and speak in her ear. Then Kautsa stroked the plump cheek of Yellow Flower's little daughter, lifted her from behind the saddle, and handed her to Eetsa. Eetsa settled the little girl behind her on her own horse. Then she looked Kaya in the eye. "Kautsa will stay here with Yellow Flower and make a birthing place for her," she said. "The rest of us will ride on to the Camas Prairie where the roots are waiting for us. Daughter, you'll stay with Kautsa. She needs your help. You can catch up with us in a few sleeps."

"Aa-heh, Eetsa," Kaya said, bending her head. Though she would do anything

her wise mother and grandmother asked
of her, Kaya felt a stab of disappointment.
Certainly she wanted Yellow Flower and
her baby to be well cared for, and Kaya
was proud to be of use. But if she stayed
behind now with Kautsa and Yellow
Flower, Kaya might miss the First Roots
celebration a second time.

When Kaya glanced up, she saw her grandmother gazing at her with gentle eyes, as if reading Kaya's mind. "There's a time for everything," Kautsa said firmly. "Now it's time for us to help Yellow Flower, Granddaughter."

Kaya watched the others ride on up the trail, Yellow Flower's daughter holding tightly to Eetsa's waist. Kautsa was looking at the swiftly flowing creek and the darkening sky. "Clouds are moving in from the west," she said. "I smell rain in the air. We must put up a shelter so that Yellow Flower and her newborn will be safe and dry. We'll make camp on that higher terrace." She pointed to a level, brush-covered terrace farther up the side of the canyon.

"Aa-heh," Kaya agreed. She knew
what they must do now. And quickly!

Kautsa on her horse led Yellow
Flower on hers to the higher terrace.
Kaya rode behind them bringing Sparks
Flying and three pack horses. After Kautsa
helped Yellow Flower from her horse, she
and Kaya went to work to build a shelter.
They quickly cut fir branches and leaned
them together to form a framework,
which they covered with tule mats. Soon
the shelter looked like a small tepee, high
enough in the center
for a woman to kneel
or sit upright.

Kautsa laid a tule mat

in the shelter. Then she and Kaya cut armfuls of bunchgrass and thickly covered the mat with it. Kautsa helped Yellow Flower creep inside the birthing place. "Now, Granddaughter," Kautsa said to Kaya, "I'll stay with Yellow Flower to assist her. But we need a fire. And we need water to brew a drink and to wash the baby after it's born."

"I'll get water and build a fire," Kaya said at once. "And care for the horses."

"Tawts!" Kautsa said. With that she ducked under the tule mat covering the entrance to the shelter and let it fall closed behind her.

Kaya sighed, wishing that she were with the others going to the root fields.

Instead, she unloaded the packs and
unsaddled the horses. Then she led the
animals back down the trail to graze on
the grassy lower terrace, hobbling the
front feet of Kautsa's mare so that the
horse couldn't wander away.
She got water, gathered wood,
and built a fire. Every single
moment that she worked,
Kaya listened hard for the
cry of a newborn baby.

hobbled horse

Dark was coming on when Kaya
finally heard the thin, sharp wail of a baby
taking its first gasp of air. *Tawts!* Kaya
thought.

After a little while Kautsa came out
of the shelter. She knelt by the fire and

wiped her hands with some bunchgrass, nodding approval of the hot drink Kaya was brewing. "Yellow Flower needs some things from her pack for her baby," Kautsa said. "She wants the little blanket of rabbit skin tanned with the fur left on. There's a buckskin diaper wrap, too, and a bundle of milkweed fluff. And don't forget the *tee-kas!*"

"I'll get those things," Kaya said. "Is the baby well?"

"You can see for yourself that he's a healthy boy," Kautsa said, and she moved aside the mat covering the entrance of the shelter.

tee-kas

Kaya gazed in at Yellow Flower

106

sitting wrapped in an elk skin, a very
small, red-faced baby with black hair held
close in her arms. Yellow Flower's braids
were rumpled, and her face and throat
were wet with sweat, but she was smiling.

"Aa-heh, he's healthy!" Kaya could
barely hear her own voice—the sight of
the beautiful new baby had stolen
her breath away.

When the baby was cared
for, Kautsa cleaned the shelter,
burying all the grass bedding.
After they'd eaten a meal of
dried salmon, she made a sleeping place
of deer hides for herself in the shelter next
to Yellow Flower. Kaya made her sleeping
place by the entrance, rolling up the tule

mat to let in fresh air.

All is well, Kaya thought as she lay listening to the rushing stream in the canyon below. The hobbled lead mare couldn't wander away, and the other horses would stay with her. The fire was carefully banked. Distant thunder rumbled in the mountains, and clouds boiled over the peaks, but no rain had fallen here. And maybe, if Yellow Flower was strong enough after a good sleep to ride again, they might even reach the Camas Prairie in time to join the First Roots ceremony. Kaya closed her eyes and was lulled to sleep by the gentle lullaby Yellow Flower sang to her son.

A shrill, piercing whistle cut into
Kaya's sleep. With a start, she sat up in
the dark shelter. The sharp whistle that
had wakened her came again. *Are the
Stick People whistling to me, sending me a
warning?* Kaya wondered. Then the shrill
sound came a third time, and Kaya realized it was the scream of a frightened
horse.

As Kaya slipped on her dress and
yanked on her moccasins, she heard the
hoofbeats of stampeding horses coming from below. There was just enough
light in the early dawn for her to make
out their shapes as they
charged up the hill.
Trying to follow the

others, the lead mare with her front feet hobbled lunged frantically behind them. Their horses were running away!

As the horses thundered by the campsite and on up the hillside, Kaya realized she had just one chance to catch the hobbled mare. As the panicked horse came near, Kaya ran to grab the mare's halter rope. There—she had it!

Kautsa had pulled on her dress and moccasins, too. "Did a mountain lion frighten the horses?" she asked. Then she gasped, "Listen! A flood! The horses heard it before we could!"

In horror, Kaya recognized the distant roar of a flash flood coming down the canyon. Had a storm in the mountains sent the crashing waters? There was no time now to think—only time to try to escape the swiftly rising flood that would soon reach their camping place.

"Cut my horse's hobble," Kautsa cried. "Be quick! I'll help Yellow Flower."

The chestnut was snorting and tossing her head wildly, trying to run after the other horses. Kaya took her knife from the bag on her belt and managed, with a quick stab, to slice through the rawhide hobble. She stroked the horse's lathered neck, trying to calm her.

Yellow Flower hurried out of the shelter after Kautsa, her baby in his teekas in her arms. "I'm troubled about my baby!" she cried.

Kaya held the halter rope firmly as Kautsa helped Yellow Flower mount the restless mare. Then Kautsa handed the tee-kas to Yellow Flower. "Go quickly," Kautsa warned. She grabbed the parfleche that held her medicine bag and cooking things and started up the trail. The way was steep, and Kautsa wasn't young, but she ran like a doe.

Kaya ran right behind Kautsa, with the mare's halter rope held tightly so that the frightened horse wouldn't bolt. Yellow Flower bent low over the mare's neck, clutching the mane with one hand and holding firmly to the tee-kas with the other.

There was no time now to think—only time to try to escape the swiftly rising flood that would soon reach their camping place.

Only when they'd gained the canyon rim did they dare come to a halt. When she could slow her breathing, Kaya looked back down the trail. In the faint light, she saw a tumult of black water crashing between the stony canyon walls. Kaya could see that the flood had carried off their shelter, their saddles, and their packs.

"All our things are gone, and our horses have run off," Kaya said in distress. "I made a mistake—I should have pastured them on higher ground!"

Kautsa set down the parfleche she carried and clasped Kaya's shoulder. "Listen to me, Granddaughter," she said firmly. "Calm yourself. It wasn't a bad mistake you made. The horses escaped the flood. And now we're safe."

"Aa-heh, it's true our things are gone," Yellow Flower added, pressing her cheek to her baby's head. "But you helped save my son."

"We're alive!" Kautsa said. "No doubt we'll find some of our things after the flood recedes. You caught my horse, and I'm sure we'll find all our horses in the hills nearby."

Kaya trusted her grandmother's wisdom, but as she thought about the stampede, she realized that she hadn't seen Steps High or Sparks Flying running with the other horses. Had they been caught by the flood?

When there was more light, Kaya
rode off on the chestnut to look for the
other horses. Kautsa had been confident
they were nearby. But the sun was high
overhead and Kaya had ridden a long way
before she sighted one of the pack horses
in a sheltered draw.

As Kaya rode into the draw, she
whistled to call her horse
to her. She rode toward the
grove of scrub pine where the
pack horse grazed. Now she
saw other horses cropping the grass under
the pines. Again Kaya whistled for Steps
High, but her horse didn't come from
the thicket. Kaya searched up and down
the draw, whistling, but Steps High was

nowhere to be found. Sparks Flying was gone, too.

Kaya felt a stronger surge of dread, but she tried to think calmly. It was true that she didn't remember seeing Steps High gallop by with the other horses—but there had been very little light. The horses had rushed by like windswept leaves, and Kaya's attention had been on catching the hobbled mare. Steps High could have passed without Kaya seeing her.

But where was Sparks Flying? Kaya knew he would have stayed with his mother at all costs. Had Sparks Flying been caught by the rising waters and swept downstream? Had Steps High tried to follow her colt and been drowned?

Kaya felt a sharp ache of fear in her chest as the other horses joined the lead horse and herded behind her out of the draw.

Kaya rode with the horses back toward Whitebird Creek. On a level place near the canyon, Kautsa had put up a lean-to of willow shrub and brush. Yellow Flower and her baby rested inside the small shelter.

"You've found our horses!" Kautsa called as Kaya rode up.

"But my horse isn't with them," Kaya said miserably. "Sparks Flying is missing, too. Where could they be, Kautsa?"

Kautsa put her warm hand on Kaya's knee and looked up into her eyes. "I think you should look for them downstream," she said. "A little while ago I heard a horse whinnying down there." She pointed toward the canyon.

As Kaya turned the chestnut, Kautsa added, "My horse is surefooted, and you can trust her. But be careful, Granddaughter!"

Kaya made her way gingerly down the wet and slippery trail. It wasn't until she'd rounded two bends that Kaya heard the whinnying Kautsa had told her about. Kaya recognized Steps High's sound. Her horse was alive! But what did her anxious whinny mean? Was she injured, or in trouble? Kaya wanted to urge on the chestnut, but she held her in as they descended over slippery stones and wet mud.

Around the next bend, Kaya saw her horse restlessly pacing alongside the swollen stream. Elated, Kaya whistled to her, but Steps High ignored the signal. All her attention was on the flooded stream.

Kaya shaded her eyes and peered across the waters. Near the far shore was a small island covered with scrub brush. There, almost hidden by the brush, was Sparks Flying! Kaya couldn't guess how he'd reached the island—perhaps he'd been on a high spot and the flood had surrounded him. Clearly Sparks Flying wanted to join his mother. But the colt was afraid to enter deep water where he couldn't see or feel the bottom. He was stranded.

Kaya dismounted the chestnut and ran to her beloved horse. As she stroked Steps High's neck, she tried to think how to reclaim the colt. She knew he wouldn't leave the island on his own. She would have to swim Steps High across the flood to the colt and somehow lead him back.

But would Steps High enter the churning waters? Kaya knew her horse would refuse unless Kaya herself felt no fear. Her father had always counseled her to act with resolve so that her horse could feel it, too. As Kaya mounted her horse, she gathered her courage. She knew Swan Circling would have been strong and afraid of nothing! *Help me now!* Kaya prayed to the Creator, *Hun-ya-wat.*

Kaya rode up the creek so that she could enter the water upstream of the island. As she rode, she studied the currents, trying to find a flow that would take them to the colt. When she was confident she'd read the river well, she turned Steps High toward the island. She dug her heels into her horse's sides. "Come on, girl! Let's go!" she cried softly. Her heart swelled as her horse walked into the icy waters. Then Steps High was swimming, and once again Kaya was one with her horse.

Steps High gathered herself and swam strongly as the flow carried them

Kaya's heart swelled as her horse walked into the icy waters.

toward the island. Kaya judged the bank at the downstream end of the island to be firm, and she guided Steps High to shore there. When the horse's hooves touched solid ground, her head came up and she clambered up the bank. Kaya saw Sparks Flying watching his mother closely as she climbed onto dry ground. Tossing his head, the colt came to join his mother and pressed against her.

The crossing had gone well, but the current was swift and branches were swept along in it. Would Sparks Flying dare follow Steps High back into the tossing waters?

Again Kaya gathered her resolve. Slowly, she rode Steps High toward the stream, the colt herding after them. Steps High walked confidently into the stream. Sparks Flying hesitated, but only for a moment. Nervously, he followed his mother. They were both swimming!

Kaya guided Steps High toward a sandy beach downstream, and the current pushed them to it. In a short time the horse and colt were safely ashore and shaking water from their manes. "Tawts, my beautiful horse!" Kaya said, stroking Steps High's wet neck. "Tawts!"

The ride upstream to the waiting chestnut mare wasn't a long one. Even the climb back out of the canyon seemed to go quickly because Kaya's heart was light and full of pride in her horse. As

It was Kautsa's praise that warmed Kaya.

they approached the camping place, Kaya saw that Kautsa had been watching from the canyon rim. She strode down the trail to meet Kaya. "I saw it all, Granddaughter," she said. "You were strong! You did just as Swan Circling would have done. Come, warm yourself at the fire."

It was Kautsa's praise that warmed Kaya.

At the campsite, Kaya saw that her grandmother had put up a second, larger lean-to next to the one where Yellow Flower rested. She'd made a fire and was cooking soup with dried fish from the parfleche she'd saved. "We're going to rest here for a bit, aren't we?" Kaya asked. She couldn't keep her disappointment in missing the

First Roots ceremony from her voice.

"Aa-heh," Kautsa said, stroking Kaya's arm with her strong hand. "We'll miss the celebration. But when it's time to dig camas bulbs, you'll be part of that celebration. I know you want to work as Swan Circling did. But everything you've done today is a gift to your people, Granddaughter."

camas plant

Kaya thought, as she had before, that her grandmother had the power to see into her heart. Kaya took a few steps away from the campsite to watch Steps High and Sparks Flying join the other horses and begin to graze contentedly. Then she looked at the lean-to where Yellow Flower rested with her baby. *I've done my best,* Kaya thought with satisfaction as she took in the quiet scene.

There were yellow *kah-keet* flowers blooming in the bunchgrass. Kaya knelt and with her knife pried up some of the plants, shaking earth from the fat roots. As she peeled and bit into the tender root, Kaya tasted the promise of new life returning to the land.

LOOKING BACK

STAYING SAFE
IN 1764

As the Nez Perce traveled with the
seasons to gather food and to hunt and
fish, they were constantly aware of the
dangers they could encounter. Fires and
floods, storms and blizzards, wild animals and enemy raiders were threats
that everyone—including children like
Kaya—knew to watch for.

From an early age, children were
taught how to live in harmony with
nature and to respect its power. They

learned about the world around them from the stories and legends their grandparents told. Kaya and her brothers and sisters did not need maps. Instead, lessons about landmarks helped them find their way as they explored the forests, rivers, and canyons of their homelands.

Exploration and playtime gave

Nez Perce children paid close attention to the stories of their elders.

children a chance to practice the skills they needed to survive in the outdoors. Little girls built miniature tepees for their dolls, which taught them how to build shelters to protect themselves and their families. Shooting games helped young warriors develop keen eyes and steady aim. Children exercised constantly by swimming, running races, riding horses,

Playtime was good practice for real-life skills, like setting up a tepee.

and playing ball games. These
tasks were great fun, but they
also helped girls and boys
develop strong bodies and sharp
minds. Everything a child learned
taught her how to think quickly, act
wisely, and keep herself safe.

The Nez Perce were careful to look
out for one another. To protect themselves against enemy raids, Kaya's
people built their tepees in a circle. They
drove their horse herds into the center of
the circle at night so that the horses could
be easily guarded. Day and night, scouts
kept watch for anyone—or anything—
that might endanger the community. In
the spring, melting snow and heavy rains

could bring a flash flood. In the summer, lightning fires were a constant threat to the dry trees and prairies. Families counted on warnings from scouts to give them time to flee from the path of destruction or prepare to fight those who threatened them.

Scouts weren't the only ones to warn of approaching danger. The Nez Perce

This painting shows the fierceness of a flash flood.

also watched and listened to the animals. Village dogs had a keen sense of smell that could warn the community of a predator before it could be seen. Horses could hear the

Village dogs were loyal protectors.

terrifying rush of a flood before people could. When Kaya heard birds sing high, whistling notes, she knew a storm was approaching.

Animals could also be dangerous. Children were taught how to recognize— and avoid—the markings of grizzly bears, mountain lions, and rattlesnakes. By knowing the ways of these wild animals, Kaya could protect herself from them. She learned that mountain lions felt threatened if someone stared into their eyes. If Kaya ever met one, she knew not to look at it directly. A threatened mountain lion was more likely to pounce!

Parents took special care to keep their babies safe. Shortly after Yellow Flower's son was born, she gently laced him into a tee-kas, or cradleboard. A Nez Perce infant spent most of his time in the cozy carrier until he was old enough to walk. Cradleboards protected babies from wandering off and getting injured. They

Avoiding wild animals was the best way for Kaya to stay safe. An adult male mountain lion could weigh more than 150 pounds!

also allowed a mother to keep her child close by while she did her daily work. She could easily wear the cradleboard on her back or prop it against a tree trunk. A loop on the back of the board made it easy to hang the tee-kas on a saddle, which was especially convenient for a people who traveled with the seasons. Nez Perce parents believed that cradleboards gave children straight backs, sturdy legs, and strong spirits. Under the loving guidance of their elders, children like Kaya grew up happy, strong, and safe.

Babies often fell asleep in their tee-kas when it was on a moving horse. The gentle motion was as soothing as being rocked.

KAYA AND THE
INJURED DOG

KAYA AND THE INJURED DOG

Kaya bent over the fresh spring *wapalwaapal* plants, cutting leaves to take to Bear Blanket. The wise old medicine woman was going to teach Kaya how to brew the plants to make a tonic. The drink would give extra energy to all who needed it. Kaya had vowed to learn as much as possible from the medicine woman so that she would be able to help her people. Now that they were camped at the Camas Prairie, Nimíipuu needed to be well and strong for the hard work of digging roots, fishing, and hunting.

As Kaya worked, she heard her young uncle Jumps Back talking to someone over the loud rush of the stream. Everyone liked Jumps Back, and Kaya smiled as she thought of his good-natured teasing. She put the leaves into her gathering bag and walked through the woods to find him.

Jumps Back was standing in a stream with Fox Tail, a bothersome boy a little older than Kaya whose teasing did *not* make her smile. They were knee-deep in the water, adding stones to a fish trap the men had built here. As Kaya approached them, her uncle's dog, *P'itiin*, came bounding to meet her. Jumps Back called the dog "girl" because he hadn't yet settled on a name that fit her.

"Tawts may-we, P'itiin!" she exclaimed as the excited dog jumped up and put her paws on Kaya's chest. Kaya stroked the dog's smooth ears and scratched behind them. P'itiin was a young dog, large and rangy, with a dark gray coat, broad chest, and legs that seemed too long for her body. One of her eyes was amber, like a wolf's, and the other eye was brown. As Kaya stroked her, she thought she saw keen intelligence

*"Tawts may-we, P'itiin!" she exlaimed as the excited dog
jumped up and put her paws on Kaya's chest.*

in the dog's mismatched eyes.

"Tawts may-we, Kaya!" Jumps Back called warmly. He splashed a silver spray of water toward her and his dog. "P'itiin, catch!" he cried.

Kaya jumped aside, but P'itiin sprang into the air and snapped at the spray, her bushy tail wagging in a circle. Then she crouched to leap into the stream, but Jumps Back quickly signaled to her, *Stay!* Instead of obeying his command, P'itiin flung herself into the water, sending a cold sheet of it over his shoulders. "P'itiin, get back!" he ordered in a stern voice.

The big dog reluctantly swam to the bank and clambered up onto it again, her tail tucked between her legs. "No more games! Mind me!" he scolded.

Kaya patted P'itiin's wet head, and the dog looked up at her with sad eyes. "Is she a good hunter?" she asked Jumps Back.

"She'll be a good one when she's older," Jumps Back said. "She's smart, but she's not dependable yet. As you saw, sometimes she obeys me, sometimes not."

"She gets into fights," Fox Tail added. "One time she fought a badger. I think she's *too* brave."

"I need more time to train her before I can trust her," Jumps Back said, testing one of the upright poles that held the fish trap firmly in place. "But now the fish are ready to give themselves for food, so I can't work with P'itiin. I have to tie her up, but she chews through the rope to come after me."

"Kaya, remember how Tatlo used to whimper when you tied him?" Fox Tail asked, looking back at her over his shoulder. "He cried like a baby!"

"Aa-heh, he wanted to go everywhere with me," Kaya murmured. It made her throat ache to think of her beloved dog, whom she had had since he was a pup. She'd given Tatlo to a visitor called Hawk Woman, who had needed his companionship and his protection more than Kaya had. But now that Hawk Woman had left with Tatlo, Kaya found herself badly missing her dog. She hadn't found another one as loving or as loyal—maybe she never would. She sank her fingers into P'itiin's thick coat, and the wet dog leaned against her leg.

The dog's warm weight reminded Kaya even more strongly of Tatlo. But she couldn't linger here when Bear Blanket was waiting for her. "I need to go back to my own work now," she said. She gave P'itiin a last pat as she turned away from the stream.

Kaya had climbed over several hills when a slight wind came up, rustling the branches of the pines. Thoughts of Tatlo

were still with her, so it took a moment
to realize that the rustling wasn't just
from the wind. Something was moving
about beneath the trees. Was that the Stick
People? Had they come to warn her about
something?

Kaya stopped and shaded her eyes
to peer into the shadows. She drew in her
breath with alarm, for there, not more
than the length of a longhouse away, was
a brown-coated grizzly bear! Swaying
slightly, it stood on its hind legs,
gazing hard toward Kaya,
its nose working to get
her scent.

Kaya's heart knocked
against her ribs. The bear

stood as tall as a man, though it wasn't heavy. It looked like a young male, perhaps on its own for the first time. In this season, bears were hungry after their long hibernation, and they became angry if they were confronted. Kaya knew she had to stay as calm as possible. She kept still and did not make eye contact with the bear. If it didn't feel threatened, the bear would go on its way. Kaya took a single, slow step backward.

As she took another deliberate backward step, P'itiin came rushing up through the woods behind her. Had the young dog sensed danger and come to defend her? The dog could be killed if it charged the bear. "P'itiin, stay!" she cried and held out her hand. But the dog ignored her command, charged past her, and rushed at the bear.

P'itiin darted around the startled bear, snarling and nipping at it. The bear turned in a circle, swatting at the dog. Kaya could see the bear's sharp teeth and long claws. Then, with a quick swipe, the bear gashed P'itiin's shoulder. With a yelp of pain, P'itiin turned from the bear and limped back to Kaya. Now the agitated bear came in angry pursuit of the dog. It was heading right toward Kaya! She tried to shout to frighten the bear, but as if in a bad dream, her cry was only a whisper.

Kaya clasped P'itiin by the scruff and began to move backward again. She knew to stay facing the bear. *Don't run!* she told herself. *If you run, the bear will give chase!* She didn't run, but moving step by steady step while her heart pounded was the hardest thing she had ever done.

Suddenly, Kaya stepped onto a fallen limb and fell to her knees. She looked up to see the bear coming closer, white foam around its mouth, its black eyes fixed on her. Again she tried to yell, and again her voice failed her. Her face was hot with fear.

P'itiin wrenched from Kaya's grasp and charged ferociously toward the bear. Growling with menace, the dog bit at the

P'itiin wrenched from Kaya's grasp and charged ferociously toward the bear.

bear's haunches. The bear slashed at the dog with its claws and teeth. Gray dog and brown bear blurred as they fought. Then, with a mighty swat, the bear caught P'itiin with its huge paw and hurled the dog through the air. The bloodied dog landed in the bunchgrass and did not move.

The fight had given Kaya a chance to get to her feet and move farther away down the trail. Instead of following her, the frustrated bear turned to a nearby fir tree and began to rip off bark in its boiling aggression. Holding her breath, Kaya kept backing away. As quickly as it had started, the agitated bear stopped its attack on the tree and moved off into the woods, ignoring Kaya and the unmoving dog.

When she was sure the bear was gone, Kaya raced back to P'itiin. The sight of bloody gashes on P'itiin's back and shoulder made her shudder. She gasped when she saw the wounded leg. P'itiin's foreleg and paw were entirely torn off. "Jumps Back!" she cried out, hoping he could hear her. This time her voice was strong.

Kaya was wrapping her gathering bag tightly around the dog's leg when Jumps Back and Fox Tail came running swiftly up the trail. Jumps Back had his knife out. "Are you hurt?" he called to Kaya. Then he saw P'itiin lying in the grass. He crouched beside Kaya, who was trying to stop the bleeding. "What happened?" he asked.

"P'itiin chased a bear," Kaya whispered. "When it came after us, she fought it."

"And now that dog is dead!" Fox Tail said with a grimace.

Kaya's hand was shaking when she pressed it to P'itiin's chest. "I can feel her heartbeat. It's a strong one."

Jumps Back shook his head in dismay. "But look at her wounds, her leg. So much blood," he said in a low voice. "I'll put her out of her pain." He drew back his knife.

As he did, P'itiin opened her eyes. She gazed up at Kaya, who bent low over her. Then P'itiin slowly lifted her remaining forepaw and placed it heavily on Kaya's trembling hand.

"Wait! She wants to live," Kaya cried. "Help me get her back to camp. Bear Blanket will give me good medicine to treat the wounds."

Jumps Back frowned deeply. Then he sheathed his knife. "Aa-heh, I'll help you," he said. "But this dog's in a very bad way. She may not make it, no matter how good Bear Blanket's medicine is."

"When the bear attacked, P'itiin did her best to save me," Kaya said. "I'll do my best to save her." As she spoke, she realized she was making a vow to do all she could to help this strong-hearted dog who had defended her.

⚘

159

Bear Blanket knew just what to do, for her wyakin had given her the power to heal both people and animals. First she washed the deepest gashes and closed them with stitches of sinew. Then she placed peeled leaves of a healing plant onto the leg and bound the poultice in place. "Swan Circling thought you could learn medicine skills that would help our people," Bear Blanket murmured to Kaya, who knelt beside her. "I believe your mentor was right. Remember, put fresh leaves on the wounds often. You know where to find these plants, don't you?"

Kaya nodded. "Ah-heh, I know where

the plants grow because you showed me."

"So I did," Bear Blanket said. "And now you know why."

When the medicine woman finished treating the wounds, she sat back on her heels and spread her wrinkled hands on her knees. "I've done all I can," she said in a low voice. Then she tipped her head and looked into Kaya's eyes. "I can see that you pay close attention to this dog," she added. "That's good. She'll tell you what she needs if you know how to listen. All creatures know what they need. Now you must be patient and prepare yourself for whatever comes."

Kaya pressed her lips tightly together. Was Bear Blanket warning her that the dog might not live? Kaya hoped with all her heart that P'itiin wouldn't tell her that she needed to journey on.

⊹

Kaya asked Jumps Back to carry P'itiin to her tepee so that she could care for the dog. All day Kaya sat beside P'itiin. Did the dog need food, water? Kaya wondered. But P'itiin lay unmoving, as if in a deep sleep. Sometimes Kaya held her hand to P'itiin's hot, dry nose to feel the soft breath there. Sometimes she saw P'itiin shudder, as if she dreamed of fighting the bear. But that was all. The big dog didn't even open her eyes when Kaya placed a sheep's-horn bowl of water beside her head.

That night Kaya slept restlessly, and before sunrise she got up and went to sit by the injured dog again. When she gently stroked P'itiin's head, the dog slowly opened her eyes. She looked up as Kaya dipped her hand into the horn bowl and dabbed some water onto the dog's dry mouth. Then P'itiin raised her head and managed to lap water from the bowl until it was dry.

"Good dog!" Kaya breathed. "Do you want more water? Do you want food?" But P'itiin laid down her head and closed her eyes again.

A shadow fell over

Kaya. She turned to find Fox Tail standing in the tepee opening, his arms crossed over his chest. "She can't get well if she won't eat," he said darkly.

"When she needs to eat, she will." Kaya tried to sound calm, but secretly she thought Fox Tail might be right. Bear Blanket had counseled patience, but surely it would take more than patience to restore the big dog's health.

"Anyway, she looks funny with only three legs," Fox Tail said with a smirk.

Kaya felt anger heat her chest. "Don't say that!" she said in a sharp voice. "You must treat P'itiin with respect. Do you understand?"

"She's just a crippled dog," Fox Tail

said, shrugging.

Kaya stood, her fists pressed into her waist. "Remember Yellow Elk? Even though he lost his hand in a hunting accident, he was still an expert horse trainer. And Speaking Rain is blind, but she's a skilled basket weaver for our people. Everyone respects her. P'itiin will be a useful dog with only three legs. You'll see."

Fox Tail raised his eyebrows. "How can she be of use when she can't even walk?" he scoffed. He ran off to join the other men and boys at the fishing site.

"She *will* walk!" Kaya cried after him. But she was more troubled than she wanted to admit. Right now the dog could barely lift her head.

Kaya lay down beside P'itiin. "Don't listen to that bothersome boy," she whispered. P'itiin's eyelids trembled as Kaya sang softly, "*Ha no nee, ha no nee.* Here's my precious one, my own dear little precious one."

As Kaya sang, Bear Blanket came into the tepee. The old woman paused and looked down kindly at her. "Ah, that's a good lullaby," she said. "My own mother sang it to me long ago."

At Bear Blanket's gentle words, Kaya's troubled feelings welled higher, and she felt tears sting her eyes. "I wish P'itiin hadn't lost her leg!" she blurted.

Bear Blanket bent over and put her hand on Kaya's shoulder. "Aa-heh, it's hard for us when an animal suffers," she said in a low voice. "But consider this, child. The dog doesn't feel sorry for herself. She accepts what comes. Let that be your lesson, Kaya."

❖

After another sleep, Kaya found P'itiin trying to sit up. Her heart lifted! The dog was nosing and sniffing at the bandages on her injured leg, and she wagged her tail in greeting when Kaya sat down next to her. P'itiin held still while Kaya unwrapped the poultice and replaced the old leaves with fresh ones. "The dog trusts you, Kaya," Bear

167

Blanket said as she entered the tepee with a basket of scraps.

"She's getting better!" Kaya exclaimed, taking the basket from the medicine woman. Kaya offered P'itiin a small piece of deer meat. Her heart lifted higher when the big dog took it from her. Kaya offered another bite, and P'itiin ate that, too.

"Hunger is a good sign," Jumps Back said in his hearty voice. He and Fox Tail had come to check on P'itiin. Jumps Back crouched and stroked P'itiin's muzzle. "Look, her eyes are bright, and her nose is damp—those are good signs, too," he said. "You have good medicine," he said respectfully to Bear Blanket.

"Aa-heh, and Kaya is using it well," Bear Blanket said. "I think that soon this dog will be on her feet again."

"And if she can walk, she'll learn to run, too," Jumps Back said firmly.

"But even if she heals well, she won't obey," Fox Tail muttered stubbornly. "What good is a dog that isn't trustworthy?" Then he looked slyly at Kaya and grinned. "If we can't trust her, I think we should call this dog 'Magpie'—like we call you, Kaya."

Magpie! That awful nickname stabbed Kaya. She'd gotten it when she hadn't taken care of her little brothers and Whipwoman had disciplined all the children for Kaya's offense. Whipwoman had said that the switching was because Kaya couldn't be trusted, that she was no more responsible than a thieving magpie. It had taken a long, long time to prove that she could be trusted, and Kaya had learned her lesson well. She didn't deserve to be called Magpie anymore!

Kaya scowled at Fox Tail. In her anger, it was hard for her to admit that this bothersome boy might be right about anything! But it came to her that he was right about this. Nimíipuu *must* be able to trust their dogs. Dogs were workers and defenders, and they had to be obedient. The people's very lives depended on it. Kaya understood that P'itiin had to do more than learn to walk again. She had to learn to obey. Kaya would have to teach P'itiin the lesson she'd learned herself—*We must all help one another*. Kaya leaned close to the dog and whispered, "I have something more than good medicine to give you, P'itiin."

Just as Bear Blanket had predicted, P'itiin was soon struggling to walk. She limped, but she was able to search for the grass she liked to eat as her own choice of medicine. When P'itiin was strong enough to join the other dogs, her limp quickly improved as she tried to keep up with them. Soon she was running, and even Fox Tail admitted that she ran as fast as she had before the bear had mauled her. Kaya was eager to begin P'itiin's training.

Each morning Kaya took P'itiin away from the village to a place where they could work without distraction. Kaya knew the commands that the dog needed to learn, and over and over she practiced the hand and voice signals with her. P'itiin was an intelligent dog. She seemed more eager to please Kaya each day they worked together.

One evening, as the shadows grew long, P'itiin followed Kaya to the stream. Suddenly, P'itiin crouched low. She gazed intently downstream and began to growl deep in her throat. Kaya could not see

When P'itiin was strong enough to join the other dogs, her limp quickly improved as she tried to keep up with them.

anything, but still P'itiin growled a warning. Then Kaya saw why. At the far bend of the stream, a bear, followed by a small cub, stepped out of the willows. P'itiin had picked up their scent.

Kaya quickly spread her hand and held it in front of P'itiin—the signal *Stay!* With the bears so close, would P'itiin obey this command?

P'itiin crouched lower. She looked up at Kaya with her piercing eyes, but she did not move. Kaya knew the dog was telling her that she wanted to go after the bears but that she chose to obey Kaya's command instead. She stayed silently at Kaya's side while the bears forded the stream and disappeared into the woods.

"Good dog!" Jumps Back said. He and Fox Tail had brought their horses to drink at the stream. They stood at the shore, watching on. "You're a patient teacher, Kaya. You two are a good pair."

"You trained her well, Kaya," Fox Tail said with grudging respect.

"You made me understand she needed training," Kaya admitted to Fox Tail.

"Kaya, would you like P'itiin to be your dog now?" Jumps Back asked.

Kaya didn't hesitate. "Aa-heh!" she exclaimed. She crouched and, with a grateful heart, pressed her face to P'itiin's soft ear.

"Tawts!" Jumps Back said. "She'll be a good friend for you. Maybe you'd like to give her a new name."

"It *won't* be Magpie," Kaya said, flashing a grin at Fox Tail. "She learned her lesson after she lost her leg, and I know she won't forget it." Kaya thought for a moment. Then she said, "I think I'll call her Three Legs. With four legs she was a brave dog, but with three legs she's both brave and trustworthy." Kaya slipped her arm over the big dog's neck and held her close as the dog licked her cheek. "You're a fine Nimíipuu dog now, Three Legs!"

LOOKING BACK

MEDICINE AND HEALING IN 1764

As the Nez Perce traveled with the seasons, they gathered a variety of plants to use for medicine.

For Kaya's people, the natural world provided everything they needed for survival. Food, shelter, and clothing came from the earth and the animals around them. Medicine was no different. The Nez Perce used many plant materials—roots, bark, leaves, flowers, seeds, and fruits—to cure illness and promote wellness. Plants provided treatments for

rashes, burns, tooth-
aches, insect bites,
and even dandruff.
The common cold was
just as bothersome in

*Boiled juniper made
a disinfecting bath.*

Kaya's time as it is today. Inhaling smoke
from dried sage was a good way to clear
clogged sinuses. Tamarack sap soothed
a sore throat. A tea of wild raspberry
leaves helped settle an upset stomach.
Young children learned about these
basic remedies, and how to prepare
them, from their parents
and grandparents.

Medicine women
with great knowledge

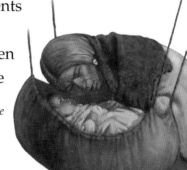

*Bear Blanket was a powerful medicine
woman for Kaya's people.*

healing plants were called *tiwata'aa* (tea-WAH-tah-at). Medicine men were called *tiweet* (tea-WAH). These healers were respected for their deep insight into human nature and spiritual matters. They were doctors who could treat illnesses of body, mind, and spirit. They knew how to combine many different plant ingredients to make the medicine a sick person needed.

Teas and tonics were carefully prepared so that the medicine would not lose its effectiveness. If someone was too sick

*Healers used a stone instrument called a **pestle** to grind plants into small pieces. The **mortar**, or bowl, usually had a stone base and woven basket sides.*

180

to drink medicine, healers fed the person drop by drop through a tube made from a hollow horsetail stem or other plant stem. Poultices, which were made from chopped or ground plants mixed with animal fat, were applied directly to wounds.

These leaves make a southing poultice for sores and scrapes.

Spiritual beliefs greatly shaped the Nez Perces' approach to medicine and healing. Healers called on their spirit helpers, or *wyakins*, to determine how to cure a person. Medicine people with bear wyakins were considered especially powerful. Bears are strong

and resilient and eat a variety of plants, herbs, and roots. They were believed to have the most knowledge about the healing power of plants, which they gave to humans.

Bears were admired for their skill in gathering plants, roots, and berries.

Healing in the Nez Perce culture varied among medicine people. Healers combined plant ingredients differently, using what they had learned from mentors, their wyakins, and their own unique experiences. Medicine people also paid close attention to their dreams and visions. They often went to the sweat house to meditate, sing, and seek guidance from their wyakins. They believed sweating cleansed their minds as well as their bodies, strengthened their

To make a purifying bath, the Nez Perce placed heated rocks inside the sweat house. Then they poured cold water over the rocks to make steam.

spirits, and helped them receive the healing knowledge they sought.

The Nez Perce honored their guardian spirits by participating in Spirit Dances. Each winter the medicine people arranged this important ceremony, and it

The feathers and fur on ceremonial clothing are often symbols of a person's wyakin.

was a time when people's wyakins drew close to their human partners and became more powerful. After feasting, anyone who had received a wyakin gathered in the longhouse, dressed in his or her finest ceremonial clothing, and danced through the night. Healers sang the sacred songs that had been given to them by their wyakins. Sharing their songs and dances strengthened the medicine men and women so that they could continue helping and healing their people.

184

Modern medicine has changed the way nearly every culture treats illness and infection. Today the Nez Perce seek treatment from doctors, nurses, and other health-care professionals. But the Nez Perce have not lost their respect for the ways of their ancestors. Traditional healing remedies are still passed on through generations, and Spirit Dances are still celebrated. This important ceremony connects modern Nimíipuu to their ancestors, helping their culture stay alive and strong.

Today, two Nimíipuu health centers in Idaho provide modern medical care as well as traditional healing.

KAYA AND THE GRANDMOTHERS

KAYA AND THE GRANDMOTHERS

Kaya rode away from the large circle of tepees, guiding Steps High with the gentle pressure of her knees. Once her horse had been headstrong and likely to buck, but she'd become steady and trustworthy. "Tawts!" Kaya murmured, enjoying Steps High's easy, rocking canter as she rode across the camas fields.

The time to dig camas was almost at

hand, and Kaya's band had joined many, many other bands here at the Weippe Prairie. In a few sleeps the lead digger would announce that it was time to begin harvesting the nourishing bulbs Nimíipuu prized so highly for food. Kaya was very eager to dig with the other girls and women, and to be part of the First Foods ceremony that honored the plants and the diggers. *This year, at last, I will take my place with the women!* Kaya thought.

As Kaya rode, she saw a tawny coyote followed by a gray one trot out of the brush, their heads tilted skyward.

Then she saw several ravens swooping and hovering over what looked like a deer carcass on the far slope. The coyotes were taking a fix on the ravens and following the birds to a meal of deer meat.

Kaya halted Steps High and scanned the brushy slope, trying to spot the coyotes' den. Her blind sister, Speaking Rain, had thought she'd heard high-pitched yips from pups when the coyotes howled together every night.

When Kaya's thoughts turned to her sister, her spirits sank. Soon Speaking Rain would leave to rejoin White Braids, the old Salish woman who had saved her life. Speaking Rain would spend part of each year with White Braids to help her, as she had vowed to do, and

White Braids

191

part of the year with her own people. As the time approached for Speaking Rain to leave, Kaya realized more and more how hard it would be to let her precious sister go. Her heart was heavy as she turned Steps High back toward the encampment.

Kaya hadn't ridden far when she saw what looked like a bundle of deerskins piled underneath a pine. Then she realized it was no pile of skins, but a small old woman in a deerskin dress resting against a large hemp bag. The elderly woman's skin was dark, and her eyes were gleaming slits in her wrinkled face. Her short, wispy braids were gray. Her thin lips turned down as she gazed at the distant slope where the coyotes were feeding. Kaya didn't recognize this old woman. Had she come to Weippe with a band from across the mountains?

Kaya knew it was disrespectful to stare, so she slipped off Steps High and walked toward the woman. Kaya could see from the design on her root bag that the old woman was a Nimíipuu. "*Tawts kulawit*," Kaya said.

When the old woman looked up at Kaya, her thin lips turned down even more. She grasped her digging stick and used it to push herself to her feet. Then she picked up her overstuffed bag. "Leave me alone, girl!" she said in a hoarse voice that sounded close to tears. "I'm looking for someone!"

Kaya was startled by the old woman's shaking voice. "Are you camped here?" she asked.

The old woman waved at Kaya with her bony hand. "I'm not camped here, girl! I'm wandering all alone! I wanted to join my cousin, but I can't find her. I have to keep wandering until I do." Abruptly she turned and walked into the thicket of pines. In only a moment she had disappeared from sight.

Kaya frowned in thought. She had never known an elder woman to journey alone without at least a grandson or granddaughter as a companion and guide. What could be wrong? Shielding her face from the prickly pine needles, Kaya ran into the thicket after the old woman. No Nimíipuu would let an elder wander off in confusion.

When she caught up to the woman, Kaya walked a step or two at her side. "Grandmother, if you're alone, come with me to my family," she said gently. "It would be an honor to have you stay with us until you find your cousin."

The old woman stopped walking. She didn't answer, but she didn't resist when Kaya took the heavy bag from her. Her narrowed black eyes stared intensely into Kaya's. After a moment she said softly, "Aa-heh, I will go with you, Little Granddaughter."

Walking with the old woman and

"Aa-heh, I will go with you, Little Granddaughter."

leading Steps High, the heavy bag hung
on the saddle, Kaya returned to her tepee.
She quickly told her mother and grandmother how she'd found the old woman
and what the woman had said.

As Kaya knew she would, Kautsa
welcomed the old woman and drew her
inside the tepee. "Please rest for a while.
We'll help you find your cousin," Kautsa
said in her warm voice. "Will you tell us
your name?"

"I am called *Taamamno*," Old
Grandmother said. "And my cousin is
Blue Grouse. We're both very old, and
I want to see her again before I die.
I think she comes here to dig roots, but
I'm troubled because I can't find her."

"Don't be troubled!" Eetsa said quickly. "Blue Grouse and her family were down at the Camas Prairie when we were there. They'll journey here to Weippe in a few sleeps."

"Aa-heh!" Old Grandmother huffed. The worry lines in her forehead seemed to soften, and she tapped Eetsa's wrist with her bony finger. "I won't be troubled then."

"Please stay with us until your cousin arrives," Kautsa said. She filled a sheep's-horn bowl with fish soup and placed the bowl in the old woman's hands.

"Kaya, you did well to bring Taamamno to us," Eetsa said. "Make sure to give her soft pieces of food that she can chew easily."

Kaya smiled to see Old Grandmother eat the warm soup gratefully. Then the old woman unpacked some things and settled comfortably onto her sleeping skins as if she had lived with Kaya's family all of her long life.

Dusk was turning to night when the men went to play the stick game. The women were chatting and the children playing when the coyotes began their nightly serenade. Their eerie, high-pitched howls wailed across the fields and echoed off the surrounding hills. The nervous dogs drew closer to the tepees, and the twins came to sit next to Old

Grandmother for comfort. "I'll tell you how I once saw a coyote save her pups from a fierce badger," she said, drawing the boys nearer. As they listened to Old Grandmother's story, they grew drowsy and soon went to their sleeping places.

Kaya lay herself down at her sleeping place next to Speaking Rain, their heads close so that they could talk, as they did every night. "Do you hear any coyote pups learning to sing?" she asked her sister.

After listening a moment, Speaking Rain whispered back, "I hear four or five coyote voices, and a few funny little squeals now and then."

"Tawts!" Kaya whispered. "Then there must be pups in the den I spotted by the fallen aspen just before I came upon Old Grandmother."

"She was wandering all alone, wasn't she?" Speaking Rain murmured thoughtfully. "That's just what I did after our enemies abandoned me on the plains. Then White Braids found me and took me home with her."

At the mention of White Braids, Kaya felt another stab of sadness at the thought of her sister leaving. "Do you miss White Braids, sister?" Kaya whispered.

Speaking Rain thought a moment. "Her hands were gentle when she braided my hair," she whispered. "She rubbed my sore feet and I rubbed her aching back. Aa-heh, I do miss her."

Kaya felt another stab of sadness at the thought of her sister leaving.

Kaya was startled to feel a sharp prick of unhappiness at her sister's words. "You'll be with White Braids again soon. Will you be glad?"

"I'll be very glad to find her well," Speaking Rain whispered.

She wants to leave us, Kaya thought. She swallowed hard. She wished she could seize her sister's hand and never let it go. But that wasn't right. She wanted to say, *I'll go with you!* But she couldn't do that. So she tried to keep her voice steady. "It's good to have Old Grandmother with us for a time. Tomorrow I'll ask her to go with me to take another look at the coyote den. If we see the pups, I'll tell you about them."

Speaking Rain didn't answer. Kaya thought her sister had fallen asleep, but then Speaking Rain whispered so softly, Kaya could barely hear her. "You have much to share with Old Grandmother," Speaking Rain murmured. "Let's go to sleep now." She turned away from Kaya and drew her buffalo hide closely around her shoulders.

The sun was high overhead when Kaya crept downwind of where she'd seen the coyote den. Old Grandmother came right at Kaya's heels. They reached a spot behind a boulder where they could see the fallen aspen without being seen.

Once in the sheltered place, they waited
silently to see if any coyotes would appear.

Suddenly, Old Grandmother leaned
forward like an eagle sighting its prey.
She pointed not at the fallen tree but at
the distant grassy slope beyond it.

Kaya looked closely. After a moment
she could see two gray ears showing
above bunchgrass moving in the wind.
Then she made out a coyote standing
poised on three feet, its head cocked. As
Kaya watched, the coyote leaped high
into the air, forepaws together, and came
down on what must have been a mouse.
In a flash it took the mouse in its mouth
and bounded down the slope toward the
aspen tree.

Tail wagging, the tawny coyote rushed out of the brush to meet the gray one. It licked the gray's muzzle and gobbled up the food.

Again Old Grandmother pointed. First one, then two more brown pups came tumbling out of the entrance to the den under the aspen. Their dark eyes and large ears looked too big for their small, wiggling bodies. The tawny coyote trotted back to meet the pups. She stood still as the little ones jumped against her, finally managing to stand up on their hind legs and latch onto her to nurse. As the pups fed, the mother looked about warily for anything that would be a danger to her little ones.

Old Grandmother threw Kaya the words, *He feeds her and she feeds the pups.*

Kaya nodded. The eager little pups with their round bellies made her smile. Kaya couldn't wait to tell Speaking Rain about what she'd seen.

When they returned to camp, Kaya found Speaking Rain sitting in the shade beside their tepee. She was weaving a small hemp basket that Kautsa had started for her. Although Speaking Rain was blind, she could weave by touch alone. Kaya laid aside her unhappy feelings from the night before and ran to kneel by her sister. "We saw them!" she said, trying to catch her breath. "There are three brown pups with great big ears! The parents take such good care of them."

Instead of urging Kaya to tell her more about the coyotes, Speaking Rain kept her attention on her work.

"Old Grandmother said that when the coyote parents go hunting, an aunt or uncle coyote guards the pups," Kaya went on. "She told me that they look after each other, just as Nimíipuu do."

Speaking Rain stopped her work and lifted her head. "Old Grandmother is a good teacher," she said slowly.

"She knows so much!" Kaya agreed.

Speaking Rain bent over her weaving

again, carefully tightening each twist of hemp cord. "Now that Old Grandmother is here, you won't miss me when I go to live with White Braids," she said bitterly.

More about White Braids. My sister doesn't think of anything now but her, Kaya thought. "And when you leave us, you won't miss me at all!" Kaya blurted out. She heard the bitterness in her own voice.

As Kaya sat back on her heels, she felt a hand on her shoulder. She looked up to see Old Grandmother standing just behind her, head cocked as she listened to what the sisters were saying. "Little Granddaughter, I've misplaced my digging stick," she said to Kaya.

"I'll help you find it," Kaya said at

once, getting to her feet. In her hurry to help Old Grandmother, she left Speaking Rain without another word—but the bitter taste of hurt feelings stayed.

The following day, Kaya and Old Grandmother went again to look for the coyote family, but they were nowhere to be seen. "The mother may have moved the pups to a new den to make sure they're safe," Old Grandmother said.

"I hope we can find the new one," Kaya said.

"In any case, the pups won't stay in their den much longer," Old Grandmother went on as they walked back to the encampment. "They're getting big now, and their time of living curled up together in a snug den is almost over. Soon they'll begin learning how to hunt on their own."

When she thought of the pups moving on, Kaya felt an unexpected pang of sadness. "The pups will miss each other then, won't they?" she asked slowly. "Do you suppose they know that time is coming?"

Old Grandmother kept walking, but she clasped Kaya's shoulder with her strong hand. "Do you know one way that we're different from coyotes, Little Granddaughter?" she asked gently.

"Creatures like coyotes don't fear change. They simply accept what comes."

"Aa-heh," Kaya agreed.

"I've lived a long time, and I've lost many friends and most of my family," Old Grandmother said, tightening her grip on Kaya's shoulder. "I've learned that it's us—people, not creatures—who are troubled by the changes we know are coming. We can imagine how we'll feel when we have to leave someone we love. And sometimes that troubles us more than we can admit. Isn't that so?"

Kaya didn't need to answer. She realized that Old Grandmother understood her well. Old Grandmother understood Speaking Rain, too. Both sisters were saddened that they'd be separated for a time, and both were afraid to admit how much.

Old Grandmother stopped walking and turned to Kaya, her dark eyes burning into Kaya's. "I've also learned that even late in life, one can find new people to love," she said.

Now Kaya thought of White Braids, and how she must be looking forward to seeing Speaking Rain again. Kaya keenly felt the warmth and wisdom of Old Grandmother's words. "Katsee-yow-yow," she said gratefully. Kaya was eager to share these wise thoughts with Speaking Rain.

She found her sister finishing the little

basket she was weaving. Speaking Rain's brow was furrowed in concentration as she tucked in the last strands of cord. Kaya knelt at her side. She wanted to tell her sister everything Old Grandmother had said, but somehow those words wouldn't come.

Instead, Kaya gently traced the rim of the basket, her forefinger brushing Speaking Rain's. "The weaving's so tight and even," Kaya said. "I think this is the best basket you've ever made."

Speaking Rain's cheeks reddened at Kaya's praise. "It's a gift for White Braids," she said in a pinched voice.

Kaya saw that her sister seemed worried—did she fear another bitter

exchange? But now Kaya felt only
gratitude at the mention of White Braids's
name. "She'll like this basket!" Kaya said.
"Maybe she'll carry her fire
starters in it."

fire starters

"Or her knife," Speaking
Rain said with a smile. "She's
very old, you know. She puts
down her knife and forgets where it is."

"The way *Pi-lah-ka* puts down his
pipe and tells us it's lost, though it's right
by his side," Kaya said. She thought a
moment, running her hand down one of
her braids. Then she quickly slipped off
the abalone hair ties and put them into
Speaking Rain's hand. "Take these
to White Braids. I want to send

abalone hair ties

215

her a gift, too."

Speaking Rain fingered the smooth circles of abalone shell. "Eetsa made these for you, didn't she?" she murmured. She placed the hair ties carefully into the little basket. "I'll tell White Braids you give them to her with respect," she said. "When we meet again, I'll bring you her thanks."

Soon the small group of men and women who were journeying to the Palouse began packing up their horses for the trip. The men would hunt and fish with their Salish friends. The women would meet their trading partners and dig camas with them. They had planned this journey so that they could take Speaking Rain to join White Braids.

Kaya was packing her sister's belongings into a large parfleche. "Here's the basket you made for White Braids," she said, tucking it in with a deerskin dress. "And here are the extra pairs of moccasins Kautsa made for you. She said you'll walk a long way before it's time to come back to us."

"Aa-heh," Speaking Rain said with a smile. "Kautsa always thinks ahead, doesn't she? Remember when she helped me to swim well?"

"She said you wouldn't be safe in a canoe unless you were a strong swimmer," Kaya said.

"I wasn't thinking about being safe," Speaking Rain said. "I was a little girl! I just wanted to play in the water. I remember Kautsa would go into the river and call my name. Of course, I couldn't see her, but I'd jump off the bank toward her voice. And she'd catch me and let me splash around with her."

"You learned fast!" Kaya said, smiling at the memory of them as little children.

"But I didn't know in which direction to swim," Speaking Rain went on. "Your job was to stand in the river near shore and call to me. Kautsa would let me go, and I'd swim toward your voice. You

218

were always waiting to grab me."

Kaya took her sister's warm hands in her own. "You and I are like the coyote pups—we've been together almost all our lives," she said. "Now we'll be apart for a while. Much will happen before we're together again. Soon I'll go on my vision quest."

"Aa-heh," Speaking Rain said, giving Kaya's hands a squeeze. "When we meet the next time, you might have a wyakin. And who knows what will have happened to me. But no matter where we are, we'll always be sisters."

When Kaya finished packing Speaking Rain's parfleche, the two walked to Speaking Rain's horse. "The others are ready to go," Kaya said, tying the parfleche onto the saddle. "They're waiting for you."

Kaya gave her sister a leg up onto her horse, then spread a deerskin across her lap. As Kautsa and Eetsa came to say good-bye, Kaya swallowed her tears. "Soon!" she said to Speaking Rain.

"Soon!" Speaking Rain repeated as her horse fell into line with the others moving away from the camp. She turned in the saddle and raised her hand. Kaya watched until the horses crested the hill and disappeared from sight. "Soon," she whispered. "We'll be together soon."

After another sleep, the lead digger, who was a respected elder, returned before sunup from checking the camas. She called out to the women and girls that it was time now to begin digging. "The roots are waiting for us!" she cried. "The roots are singing!"

For several days the women who

were selected to be the First Diggers had been cleansing themselves and fasting so that they'd be ready to dig again. As the eastern sky began to glow pink with the rising sun, the First Diggers put on the clothes they had worn last year so that the roots would recognize them. Old Grandmother and Kaya watched as Kautsa and Eetsa put on their white deerskin dresses decorated with elk's teeth and beads, and picked up their root bags and digging sticks.

Kaya smoothed the long fringe on the sleeves of her mother's beautiful dress. She knelt and smoothed the fringe on the hem, too. "Eetsa…" she murmured.

"I know, daughter," Eetsa said kindly, motioning for Kaya to get to her feet again. "I think you're longing to come with me now, as I once longed to join Kautsa as a First Digger. Isn't that so?"

Kaya nodded. Her mother had read her thoughts well.

Eetsa turned and gave Kautsa a deep look. "And I remember my mother told me my time would come soon enough."

Kautsa smiled, then put her warm hand on Kaya's shoulder. "You're growing into a strong young woman," she said approvingly. "After the First Roots feast, we'll all be digging together."

Then Old Grandmother stepped forward. She placed her digging stick

"I want you all to be proud of me," Kaya said softly.

into Kaya's hands. "My digging stick is old and it isn't very pretty, but it's very strong," she said. "I'd like you to use it when you start digging. I was a good digger when I was younger."

Kaya ran her hand down the shaft of the digging stick and tested the point. The syringa wood was smooth, and the fire-hardened point was sharp. "Katsee-yow-yow," she said. "I'll work hard." As she looked at Eetsa, Kautsa, and Old Grandmother, her thoughts turned to her mentor, Swan Circling, who'd had confidence that Kaya would become strong and trustworthy. "I want you all to be proud of me," she said softly.

Kaya and the others followed the

First Diggers, who were gathering in a circle to pray before they set out for the fields. Kaya gazed at the solemn faces of the diggers with their strong arms and straight backs. The women lifted their voices in a prayer song praising Hun-ya-wat and thanking Him for His many gifts to the Nimíipuu. As Kaya listened, she rejoiced that soon she would work with these powerful women, who labored every day of their lives to care for their people.

LOOKING BACK

GATHERING FOOD
IN 1764

Before camas was ready to harvest, the lily-like plants burst into bloom.

When summer became hot and dry,
Kaya and her people traveled to Weippe
Prairie, where the air was cooler.
They set up camp by the camas
meadows and spent several
months digging the fresh roots
that were so important to their
survival. Though much of the
Nez Perce's diet consisted of

*Camas bulbs could be boiled, but they were
usually baked in an underground oven.*

salmon, buffalo, and other meat that the men and boys fished and hunted for, it was roots and berries, gathered by women and girls, that provided more than half of their nourishment. This work was deeply respected by everyone. Women were honored for feeding the people, and they were considered equal in status to the men because of their contributions. Kaya was eager to take up her digging stick and root bag and join the other women in the camas fields. More than any-thing, she wanted

While Kaya waited for the camas plants to finish flowering, she finished weaving her very own root bag.

to help her people stay strong and healthy.

Though the Nez Perce dug many different types of roots, camas was especially important because it was the main staple of their winter diet. Roots gathered in the summer were baked in underground pits, dried, and stored in large baskets. All the women worked hard to gather enough roots to last through the long, harsh winter. Running out of stored camas before the new spring roots were ready to dig was a serious threat to the Nez

Berries were also a staple of the Nez Perce diet. Women and girls gathered huckleberries, elderberries, serviceberries, and other berries that grew wild along the mountainsides.

Perce's survival. The women prepared for each new digging season by praying and fasting. They cleansed themselves and cleared their minds of any bad thoughts that would make the roots hide themselves.

When the first roots of the season were gathered, the Nez Perce held a special ceremony called the *First Roots feast*. They gave thanks to their Creator, *Hun-ya-wat*, for the food He provided,

Friends and family gather to celebrate the first roots of the season as well as the women who gather them.

Nimíipuu visited with old friends and made new ones at Weippe Prairie.

and they honored the women who gathered it. The celebration continued for up to a week with dancing, trading, and games. Even though root digging was hard, hot work, the gathering of many bands at Weippe Prairie was a happy social time.

Girls looked forward to another food

ceremony called the *first foods feast*. The first time a girl gathered food as a working member of the group, she had the honor of serving that food to the eldest woman of the village at a feast called *ta-la-pósa*. The word means "to worship," and people came to honor the first work the girl was contributing to her people. During the ceremony, the girl did not eat, to show that she was now a provider.

The first foods feast was a significant rite of passage. Everyone in the village was invited, and prominent members of the band gave speeches to praise and encourage

Boys were also honored with a feast the first time they contributed fish or game to the people.

the girl's work. Elders were the most respected members of the band, so they spoke first. Their words were believed to give children the power to become successful in later life.

Today, some women still gather berries and dig roots. Though camas is no longer the staple of the Nez Perce diet, it's often eaten on special occasions. Modern children continue to learn how important traditional foods, and the women who gathered

Grandmothers watched their granddaughters closely to see what talents they possessed. Those talents were respected and nurtured as the children grew.

them, were to the survival of their people. Girls Kaya's age still have opportunities to be providers and leaders in their communities. Nez Perce women are members of tribal councils, prominent spiritual leaders, teachers, artists, and doctors. Their talents continue to contribute to the Nez Perce culture, helping the people stay strong and healthy.

Modern Nimíipuu still gather at traditional digging fields to enjoy time with family and friends.

In these stories, Nez Perce words are spelled so that English readers can pronounce them. After each word below, you'll also see how the word is spelled by the Nez Perce people, how they pronounce the word, and what it means.

aa-heh/'éehe *(AA-heh)*—yes, that's right

Eetsa/Iice *(EET-sah)*—Mother

Hun-ya-wat/Hanyaw'áat *(hun-yah-WAHT)*—the Creator

kah-keet/qeqiit *(cak-TEAT)*—wild potato

katsee-yow-yow/qe'ci'yew'yew' *(KAHT-see-yow-yow)*—thank you

Kautsa/Qaaca'c *(KOUT-sah)*—grandmother from mother's side

Kaya'aton'my' *(ky-YAAH-a-ton-my)*—she who arranges rocks

Nimíipuu *(nee-MEE-poo)*—The People; known today as the Nez Perce

Pi-lah-ka/Piláqá *(pee-LAH-kah)*—grandfather from mother's side

p'itiin/pit'iin' *(pit-TEEN)*—girl

236

taamamno/tamámno *(tah-MUM-no)*—hummingbird

tawts/ta'c *(TAWTS)*—good

tawts kulawit/ta'c kuleewit *(TAWTS COO-law-at)*—good
evening

tawts may-we/ta'c méeywi *(TAWTS MAY-wee)*—good
morning

tee-kas/tikée's *(tee-KAHS)*—baby board, or cradleboard

wah-tu/weet'u *(wah-TOO)*—no

wapalwaapal *(WAH-pul-WAAH-pul)*—western yarrow, a
plant that helps stop bleeding

wyakin/wéeyekin *(WHY-ah-kin)*—guardian spirit

JANET SHAW

When I was writing the stories about Kaya and her people, Nez Perce women and men took me through their country in what is now Idaho. We went down the Snake River and up onto the Buffalo Trail, where I saw deer and elk and observed a wolf pack. Best of all, in a wooded glen I saw a mare and her newborn foal in a herd of Appaloosa horses. They looked just like Steps High and her foal. Kaya didn't come alive for me until I met her people and journeyed through her homeland.

238

BILL FARNSWORTH

Bill Farnsworth has spent the last twenty-three years creating paintings for magazines, advertisements, children's books, and fine art commissions of portraits and landscapes. He says, "Every piece of art I create is a moment in time that reflects how I feel about the subject."

Mr. Farnsworth teaches part time at the Ringling School of Art. He lives in Venice, Florida, with his wife, Debbie, and daughters, Allison and Caitlin.

239

American Girl extends its deepest appreciation to the advisory board that authenticated Kaya's stories:

Lillian A. Ackerman, Associate Professor, Adjunct, Department of Anthropology, Washington State University

Vivian Adams, Yakama Tribal Member, former Curator of Native Heritage, High Desert Museum

Rodney Cawston, Colville Confederated Tribes

Constance G. Evans, Retired IHS Family Nurse Practitioner and former Nez Perce Language Assistant/Instructor, Lewis-Clark State College

Diane Mallickan, Park Ranger/Cultural Interpreter, Nez Perce National Historic Park

Ann McCormack, Cultural Arts Coordinator, Nez Perce Tribe

Frances Paisano, Nez Perce Tribal Elder, Retired Educator

Rosa Yearout, Nez Perce Tribal Elder, M-Y Sweetwater Appaloosa Ranch